Withdrawn Stock
BCP Libraries

TO BE A

CAT

www.**kidsatrandomhouse**.co.uk

Also by Matt Haig:

Shadow Forest
(*Winner of the Gold Smarties Award
and the Blue Peter Book of the Year Award*)
The Runaway Troll

For adults:
The Dead Fathers Club
The Last Family in England
The Possession of Mr Cave
The Radleys

TO BE A CAT

MATT HAIG

Illustrated by Pete Williamson

THE BODLEY HEAD

TO BE A CAT

A BODLEY HEAD BOOK 978 0 370 33206 2

Published in Great Britain by The Bodley Head,
an imprint of Random House Children's Books
A Random House Group Company

This edition published 2012

1 3 5 7 9 10 8 6 4 2

The Random House Group Limited supports the Forest Stewardship Council
(FSC®), the leading international forest certification organization. Our books
carrying the FSC label are printed on FSC®-certified paper. FSC is the only
forest certification scheme endorsed by the leading environmental organizations,
including Greenpeace. Our paper procurement policy can be found at
www.randomhouse.co.uk/environment.

Set in Baskerville MT 15/21pt by Falcon Graphic Art

RANDOM HOUSE CHILDREN'S BOOKS
61–63 Uxbridge Road, London W5 5SA

www.**kids**at**randomhouse**.co.uk
www.**totallyrandombooks**.co.uk
www.**randomhouse**.co.uk

Addresses for companies within The Random House Group Limited can be
found at: www.randomhouse.co.uk/offices.htm

THE RANDOM HOUSE GROUP Limited Reg. No. 954009

A CIP catalogue record for this book is available from the British Library.

Printed and bound by CPI Group (UK) Ltd, Croydon, CR0 4YY

For the humans Andrea, Lucas and Pearl.
And for the cats I have known, and wanted to be –
Lapsang, Typhoo, Professor Higgins, Sprite, Angus,
Poppy and, of course, Maurice.

Be careful what you wish for
– Old saying, said by miserable people everywhere

A Secret

Here is a secret I shouldn't really tell you, but I will because I just can't help it. It's too big. Too good. OK, sit down, get ready, brace yourself, have some emergency chocolate handy. Squeeze a big cushion. Here it is:

Cats are magic.

That's right.

Cats. They're magic.

They have powers you and I can only dream of having.

But even as I tell you this I can see what you are thinking. You're thinking, *No, they don't. Cats are just cute little pets who sleep next to radiators all day long.*

To which I would say – *That's just what they want you to think.* And now you're thinking, *These are just words in a story written by some author with a boring name, and authors aren't to be trusted one bit because they tell lies for a living.*

And you're a little bit right.

But stories aren't always lies. They are things stored in all our imaginations – hence the name *stories* – and it is the author's job to point them out. And some of the things we imagine are more true than the facts we learn in maths; it's just a different kind of truth to $76 - 15 = 61$.

So yes, every cat who ever prowled the earth is capable of doing some very special things. Such as:

1. The ability to understand a thousand different animal languages (including gerbil, antelope and the ridiculously complicated goldfish).
2. Fence-balancing.
3. The capability of napping anywhere – laps, kitchen floors, on top of TVs when the theme tune to the news is blaring at full volume.
4. Smelling sardines from two miles away.
5. Purring. (Trust me, that is magic.)
6. The capacity, via their whiskers, to sense approaching dogs.
7. *****_******* ***_*** *************.

Let's stop here, at number seven. OK, one to six seem quite ordinary. You might know that cats do some of these things, even if you've never understood it as magic before. But if you see magic often enough it starts to look normal. And don't get me wrong, this is by no means the end of the list. Indeed, the list is so long that it would fill ten whole books the size of this one, and your eyes would be bleeding by the time you got to 9,080,652: 'Radiator radar'.

But number seven is a good place to stop. This seventh power is the most important one, at least for the tale I am about to tell you. (Although, if you want to read a book about radiator-detecting felines I highly recommend A. B. Crumb's exceptional *Warmpaws*, which is by far the best of its type.)

Also, you might be wondering what *****-******* ***-*** ************ actually is. Well, we'll get to that. Don't be too greedy. You can have enough secrets in one chapter, you know. The truth is, number seven is quite a big deal. I had to put asterisks instead of the actual letters because I've got to be careful how I tell you this. If I just came out with it right now you'd either not believe me or you'd have too much understanding all at once and you wouldn't understand the hidden dangers.

So don't worry, I'll tell you about it in good time.

What I will say is that those humans who get to experience it come to understand its terrible and often deadly effects and certainly never look at a cat in the same way again. One of those poor souls was an unfortunate boy called Barney Willow, and he's waiting for you on the very next page.

Barney Willow

Barney wasn't the happiest boy in the world, but he wasn't the unhappiest, either. There was a boy in New Zealand called Dirk Drudge who was even unhappier following a lightning strike and a nasty accident involving a poisonous spider and a toilet, but this isn't his story. Anyway, Barney lived with his mum in Blandford, Blandfordshire, which is such a boring place you definitely won't have heard of it.

Looks-wise, Barney was about your height but with a few more freckles. His ears stuck out a bit, as though his head was a portable unit which required handles on either side. He also had slightly curly hair which never did as it was told, and the kind of face old ladies liked to pinch a little too hard, for some reason, as if he was five, not about to turn twelve. These same old ladies often used to ask him, 'Are you lost?' when he wasn't. He just had that look about him.

Barney's best – OK, *only* – friend, Rissa, was a girl,

but they were on such good terms he never brought up the subject.

His parents were divorced.

'It wouldn't have been fair on you, Barney,' his mum used to say, 'if we'd stayed together arguing like cats and dogs.'

But that's not the horrible part. In fact, I'm going to go now and let the story tell you all that stuff. It's just too emotional for an author sometimes.

The horrible part was this: two hundred and eleven days ago (Barney was counting) his dad disappeared altogether. He'd never seen him since, except in dreams.

Indeed, Barney dreamed about his dad a lot.

He was dreaming about him right now.

They were at a pizza restaurant, just him and Dad, exactly like they'd been the last time he'd seen him.

'This is nice pizza,' his dad said.

'Dad, I don't want to talk about the pizza. I want to talk about you.'

'*Really* nice pizza.'

But then a giant tongue came down from the ceiling, flicking the table and the pizzas over, and rubbing its roughness against Barney's face.

And then Barney woke up. Vaguely remembered it was his birthday.

'No, Guster, get off!'

Guster was his dog. A King Charles spaniel whom his dad had found at a rescue centre, and who had given Barney absolutely no hint of his plan to wake him up every morning by jumping on his bed and licking his whole face until it was sticky with dog saliva.

'Guster, please! I'm still asleep!'

Of course, this wasn't true. It was just wishful thinking. But Barney spent his whole life wishful thinking, which was his trouble, as you'll soon find out.

Today was his twelfth birthday, but that wasn't something he was too excited about. After all, this was the first birthday he'd had without his dad being there.

If that wasn't bad enough it was also the first birthday he'd had at his rubbish new school. And school meant Miss Whipmire, the head teacher from hell. He didn't know if that was her exact address, but it definitely shared the same postcode. Anyway, Miss Whipmire was horrible. And she hated every single pupil at Blandford High. 'I see my job as a gardener,' she'd once said in assembly. 'And you are the weeds. My job is to cut you down and pull you up and make everything as quiet and perfect as it would be if the school had no horrible children in it.' But while Miss Whipmire didn't like any child, she seemed to hate Barney even more than the others.

Only last week he had got into trouble when he and Gavin Needle had been sent to her office.

Gavin Needle had stuck a drawing pin on Barney's seat, and he had sat down and yelped in pain. Their geography teacher had told them both to go to Miss Whipmire's office. But when they got there Miss Whipmire sent Gavin back to class and concentrated all her evilness on Barney. If it had been anyone else's behind that had been pin-punctured then Miss Whipmire would have delighted in the opportunity to humiliate Gavin (or 'Weedle', as she called him), but not when that behind belonged to Barney.

Which meant Gavin was free to carry on sticking drawing pins on Barney's chair. Or, if he had no drawing pins, just pulling back the chair seconds before Barney sat down. Oh yes, Gavin had read the 'Chair Torture' chapter in *The Bully's Handbook* at least a hundred times.

So, between Miss Whipmire and Gavin Needle, Barney didn't want to think about what lay in store today. He just wanted to keep his eyes closed and pretend it was still night-time. Which was hard, given that his face was being licked by a rough, wet tongue.

Barney pulled the duvet over his head but even that didn't stop the spaniel, whose narrow nose and long tongue nuzzled into the darkness to find him.

And then, as every morning, his mum urged him out of bed.

'Come on, Barney! I know it's your birthday but it's time to get up. I'm going to be late for the library!'

So Barney got out of bed, watched his mum whirling about at her normal hyper-speed. Then he washed, brushed and dressed everything that needed to be washed, brushed and dressed, and went downstairs.

In the hallway Guster nudged against his knees. Barney looked down and saw his dog's brown floppy ears and rather proud, upturned nose.

'All right, boy. Walkies.'

To Be a Cat

'If you really want a dog, you must be prepared to look after it,' Barney's mum had told him before they had brought Guster home from the dog rescue centre five years ago. 'And that means walking it twice a day.'

To be honest, Barney didn't mind taking Guster for walks. It was often the nicest bit of the day, especially when the weather was behaving itself. Today, though, it began to rain as Barney sat on the park bench waiting for Guster to do his business. Harsh, heavy rain which blatantly ignored the fact that Barney hadn't brought an umbrella.

'Some birthday,' Barney mumbled as he clipped the lead back onto Guster's collar.

He knew he was feeling sorry for himself, but he couldn't help it.

On his way home, he passed a house on Friary Road with an old, silver-haired cat sitting in the window, snug and smug in the warmth. *To be a cat*, he thought to himself. *That would be an easy life.*

No school.

No Gavin Needle.

No need to be woken before seven in the morning.

Total freedom. And, unlike dogs, you don't even have to go out in the rain.

As he was thinking all this the cat turned towards him, and Barney realized it was the same cat he often saw staring out at him from this house. The cat only had one eye. Its other eye socket was stitched up with a white thread so thick Barney could see it from the street.

Guster saw the cat too, yanked hard on the lead and began yapping.

'Come on, Guster, stop being stupid. You're not fooling anyone.'

Just before arriving home Barney bumped into the postman. 'Anything for number seventeen?' he asked.

The postman had a look through the bundles of post. 'Oh yes. Yes, there is.'

And Barney took the envelopes and quickly shuffled through them. A birthday card from Aunt Celia was there amid the brown-enveloped bills, but there was nothing from his dad. He knew it was unlikely, and it was stupid to expect anything, to hope for a glimpse of that handwriting he knew as well as his own.

But if his dad was still alive Barney had been sure that his birthday was the most likely day he'd make contact.

But no. Nothing.

'Oh, more bills,' sighed his mum, receiving the bundle from her son.

'Never mind, Mum,' said Barney, trying to sound convincing.

His mum pecked him on the cheek, in fast-forward, then shot out the door. 'I'll be late tonight,' she said. 'There's a meeting. I'll be back around sevenish. But there's some salad in the fridge if you get hungry.'

Salad?!

On his birthday!

You know, he wasn't expecting a ten-course meal followed by a hot-air balloon ride, or anything, but maybe he'd expected a little bit more than a night on his own eating lettuce and doing his homework.

He watched his mum get into the Mini and couldn't help feeling she wasn't really a person any more. She was just a blur, always on the move and only stopping every now and then for a sigh.

She drove away.

And Barney stood on the doorstep, watching the rain and wishing his dad was there.

'Oi, cheer up, Willow, you're only twelve,' came a voice. 'No reason to start looking like an adult already.'

The voice was Rissa Fairweather's. Barney looked up and saw his best friend standing there, tall and grinning, and with an umbrella spotted like a leopard.

'Hi, Rissa,' he said, smiling for the first time that morning.

Rissa Fairweather

'Made it myself,' said Rissa, handing Barney a birthday card. 'You know, gets a bit boring sometimes on the barge on a cloudy night.'

Oh, yes, dear readers. I should tell you – and I must break my promise and interrupt again (I'm not good with promises, they make me itchy) – that Barney's best friend was a little bit unusual. She really did live on a barge. And she didn't have a TV. She had a telescope instead, and spent most of her nights watching the sky, looking for star constellations (until he met Rissa, Barney thought Orion's Belt was an item of clothing).

You might think that such a girl would get picked on at school. No TV. Strange hobby. Lives on a boat. Hair like a pirate. And at least a foot taller than any other person in her year.

But no.

Unlike Barney, for whom Gavin Needle and his friends made life a daily torment, Rissa was one

hundred per cent bully-proof. Do you want to know her secret? She genuinely didn't *care* what people said about her. In fact, she quite enjoyed it if people called her names. It made her feel shiny inside.

On her first day at Blandford she'd had a few people shout 'Weirdo' and 'Barge girl' in her direction, but that just made her smile. She always thought of something her mum said: 'If people pick on you, they see something inside you that they are scared of. Something special, which they might not have, which shines out of you like a jewel.'

If anyone ever *did* pick on her, Rissa always imagined a shining emerald getting another polish. Or, if she was really bothered about something, she'd say the word 'marmalade' (her favourite food).

It might sound silly, but that's what her dad had suggested, and it worked for her.

Anyway, I'm rambling.

You are wondering what all this has to do with magic cats, aren't you? I can see it in your face.

Well, you'll get to that in a minute. Or a hundred minutes. It depends how fast you read. But right now let's go back to the tale and learn more about Barney's totally terrible birthday at school. In fact, let's grab a timetable. *Hasta luego.*

Barney's Totally Terrible
Birthday Timetable

8.30 a.m.–9 a.m.
Barney walked with Rissa to school. He got splashed by the school bus. Everyone on the bus looked out of the window and laughed at him, including Gavin Needle, who shouted, 'Mind the puddle!' and laughed as if he'd just told The Best Joke Ever.

9 a.m.–9.30 a.m.
The deputy head, Mr Waffler, broke his own World's Most Boring Assembly record for the third time in a year, with a talk about the various types of moss he discovered while on holiday in the Lake District.

9.30 a.m.–10.30 a.m.
Maths. (As in, *maths*.)

10.30 a.m.–11 a.m.

Break. In which a perfectly nice conversation with Rissa was interrupted by Gavin Needle shouting, 'Is that your girlfriend?' To which Barney decided to foolishly answer, 'No,' for Gavin to shout back, 'I wasn't talking to you. I was talking to Rissa.' And Barney was left with nothing to say except, 'Funny,' in a rather quiet voice.

11 a.m.–midday

Geography. In which Gavin displayed his usual virtuosity by pulling Barney's chair back while Mrs Fossil talked about volcanoes.

Midday–1 p.m.

Barney spent lunch hour eating overcooked bolognese and undercooked spaghetti. He chatted to Rissa as she explained some stuff about stars and about how the sun – our closest star – was growing all the time and would one day turn into something called a red giant and destroy the earth. Which would have been interesting if Barney hadn't felt a different kind of heat – that caused by Miss Whipmire's glare – burning the back of his neck as she stared at him through the little window in the canteen door.

1 p.m.–2 p.m.

English. During which Mr Waffler waffled about Barney's poor marks. ('Such a shame for a boy of such fine imagination.')

2 p.m.–3 p.m.

IT. In which Gavin and his friends seemed to be planning something, as they visited the catchily-titled website: www.waystogetpeoplecalledbarneywillowin-totrouble.com.

3 p.m.–4 p.m.

French. During which Gavin and his friends were mysteriously absent. At about 3 p.m. Barney went to the toilet. Then, while he was walking along the corridor, the fire alarm went off. Barney turned to see Miss Whipmire glaring at him.

'You are in big trouble, Barney Willow!'

'It wasn't me! You can see I'm nowhere near a fire alarm.'

But ten minutes later, with everyone lined up on the field, Miss Whipmire walked over to Barney Willow and harshly whispered into his ear the three most terrifying words in the universe.

'My office. *Now.*'

Miss Whipmire's Pen Pot

Barney could smell fish. The fish smell seemed to be coming from Miss Whipmire's desk, but there was nothing on there except a typed letter and a pen pot.

It was a weird-looking pen pot. Black with two holes in it, staring at him like eyes. But not fish eyes.

Miss Whipmire had told him to wait there while she went outside to check something.

He knew when she came back he was going to be in big trouble. And he knew the letter on the desk would tell him how much. He stood up, leaned forward and tried to have a look at the upside-down writing.

Dear Mrs Willow,

I am writing to inform you that your son, Barney, is a—

But that was as much as he could read before he heard the door behind him. It opened, it closed, the click of the latch sounding as grim as a last nail hammered into a coffin.

Barney shot back down into his seat. He didn't dare turn round, even though Miss Whipmire stayed behind him for a moment, saying nothing.

He pictured her standing there, watching him with disgust. Her eyes, bulging with evil, staring over her glasses towards the back of his head.

Barney wished he could start the day again, wished that when he had felt Guster's sandpaper tongue he had pulled the duvet back over his head and just stayed there.

That was the thing with Barney these days.

He did a lot of wishing.

Miss Whipmire walked round the front of her desk and sat down, ready to talk about the fire alarm.

'So, Barney Willow,' she said in her crisp, dry voice. 'Barney Willow, Barney Willow, Barney Willow . . . *always* Barney Willow . . . Now, tell me, why did you set off the fire alarm?'

Barney sat uneasily in his chair. He looked again at the strange pen pot on the desk. 'I didn't do it.'

Miss Whipmire took a deep breath and sat perfectly

upright in her chair. She was looking cross. But she always did; her mouth a small tight 'O', her black hair scraped back so tightly it raised her thin eyebrows to such a height that the wide, angry eyes beneath them looked like they might roll out onto the desk, knocking off the tiny glasses that sat pointlessly at the end of her nose.

'You didn't do it?' Her voice was ominous. 'Of course. You never *do it*, Barney, do you? You never disrupt assembly, or write graffiti in the toilets, or pick fights with Gavin Needle.'

That last lie was too much. Barney couldn't stop himself objecting. 'Gavin had put a drawing pin on my seat. As he always does. It's his idea of a joke. Just like giving me a dead arm as he walks past is his idea of a joke. He's a bully. He's always been a bully.'

For a moment Miss Whipmire seemed to be agreeing with him. She certainly didn't like Gavin Needle. And as Barney spoke her head seemed to nod, and a distant sadness arrived in her eyes. But she soon snapped out of it. She hated Barney – that was clear. Not just because of today and last week, but from all those other times too. For instance:

He had only been at this school for half a year but he had been thrown out of about ten of her assemblies. Once for saying 'Ow!' when Gavin had clipped his ear, but all the other times it had been for a noise someone else had made.

Like when Alfie Croker had giggled.

('Out, Barney Willow, we do not tolerate giggling in this school!')

Or when Lottie Lewis, sitting miles away, had sneezed.

('Barney Willow, if you refuse to control your nose get out of this hall right now . . . RIGHT! Now!')

Or when Mr Waffler made a yawning sound.

('Oh, Barney Willow, I'm boring you, am I? Well, perhaps you'd be more interested in detention!')

He'd once even got in trouble in the playground for reading his favourite book, *The Water Babies* by Charles Kingsley. ('Reading at break! How dare you? Come to my office . . .')

'I'm not here to talk about Gavin,' Miss Whipmire now said. 'Or drawing pins. I am here to talk about you. What *is* it? Your problem?' She smiled wickedly. 'Missing Daddy?'

Barney felt a surge of anger rise inside, like molten rock. 'You can't say that!'

'Oh, but I just did. And, frankly, I don't blame him. I think I would have run away if I'd had you as a son.'

'He didn't run away.' Barney felt a tear rising. Closed his eyes, locked it up.

'Oh, really? So what happened?'

Course, Barney couldn't answer this. After all, his dad hadn't been living with Barney at the time. Barney's parents had divorced a year before, and so his dad lived alone in a flat, seeing Barney only on Saturdays for outings to the zoo and pizza restaurants which never felt as much fun as they should have been.

Then, last summer, he just vanished.

Zip. Poof. Gone. Not a trace.

27

Leaving a hole big enough for a million questions but not one single answer.

The police couldn't solve it.

The *Blandford Gazette* had run an article displaying his dad's face with a big question mark.

And Barney's mum began acting very weirdly, as though someone had just pressed a fast-forward button and made her go at triple-speed.

Oh, and that was when Barney started having the dreams. Sometimes just him and his dad in the pizza restaurant like the one this morning. But other times they'd be nightmares. He'd see his dad screaming in agony, holding a hand over his eye, blood leaking through his fingers.

Soon afterwards, Barney began at Blandford High, and from his very first week there Miss Whipmire began picking on him, blaming him for other people's giggles in assemblies or graffiti that wasn't in his handwriting.

'What happened to your daddy?' Miss Whipmire said, repeating her question.

'No one knows.'

She gave a little laugh that came out of her nose. 'Someone always *knows*. You're just not looking in the right place. But then, you're not exactly what one might call bright, are you? I've seen the marks you're getting.'

The head teacher stood up, went over to her filing cabinet and took out some kind of form. 'Yes, you're the lowest in your year. The most stupid eleven-year-old in the school.'

'Twelve,' Barney said. 'It's my birthday today.'

Miss Whipmire shrugged, as if Barney's age and birthday were the two most trivial things in the world.

'Any idea why your marks are so low?'

Of course, Barney had an idea. A few months ago he'd been getting As and Bs for his homework. Now he was lucky to get an F, even though he was working harder than ever.

'It might be because *you* mark all my homework,' Barney ventured. 'When I was like all the other kids, getting marked by normal teachers, I did OK.'

Miss Whipmire looked furious. 'I have high standards. That is all.'

'I just think it's—'

Miss Whipmire shut the filing cabinet, turned. '*Silence*. This is my office. You do not so much as breathe in here unless I tell you to.' And she leaned and whispered into his ear. 'Do you understand?'

Barney nodded, staring up at a calendar on the wall.

Above the month of February was a picture of a cat. A white fluffy Persian stretched out in the sun. Miss Whipmire saw Barney looking and seemed pleased. The whisper in his ear softened. 'That would be the life, wouldn't it? To be a cat, lying out in the sun, without all those human worries . . .'

Barney felt almost hypnotized by her words. *To be free! To not have any more scary meetings in Miss Whipmire's office! To have no more nightmares! To not go to the same school as Gavin Needle!*

Miss Whipmire picked up the letter on the desk. 'But you are not. You are *you*.' And then she placed the letter in an envelope that was lying beneath it. 'And this is for your mother.'

Barney panicked. The last letter home had made his mum cry. And by cry, I mean wail. And by wail, I mean sitting on the stairs clinging onto the banister and rocking back and forth. He'd promised it would be the last time, even though he had only shouted at Gavin because of a drawing pin (and Miss Whipmire *knew* that).

'In it,' said Miss Whipmire, 'I explain that this is the last letter home you get before you are expelled. If you step so much as a *whisker* out of line, you are finished here.'

'*Expelled?* But I've done nothing wrong!'

Miss Whipmire smiled. 'Your mother will be very upset, I should imagine. You see, I am a mother too. Not many people know that about me. Anyway, I understand all too well the pains of motherhood.'

Barney took the envelope, his hands trembling as he saw the tall, elegant writing: *Mrs Willow.* The last, looping stroke of the 'W' flicked up like a tail. Barney felt sick. The faint smell of fish mixed with his panic, making his stomach churn.

Miss Whipmire gestured to the door, signalling for Barney to leave. 'And you'd better give it to her. I'll be phoning to check.'

Barney stared one last time at the cat calendar.

Miss Whipmire gave a little wave as he left. 'Miaow,' she told him with a sinister chuckle.

Barney turned at the door. 'Why are you doing this?'

Miss Whipmire pretended to think. 'I don't know,' she said, with slow and sinister delight. 'I just despise you. Of course, all children have a right to be despised, but with you it just comes too easily. Isn't that enough? Oh, and remember, don't run along to your teachers to moan about how unfair I'm being. It didn't work last time, did it? Everyone knows I've turned this school around! It has the best results in the whole of Blandfordshire. Well, apart from yours, obviously . . . Now, if you would leave and go back to your pathetic little existence, well, that would be lovely.'

Barney left the room as the bell went. Pupils rushed out of their classes, happy to be going home. He saw Gavin Needle and his friends, laughing in his direction.

'Sorry, Barney,' Gavin whispered. 'I really thought there was a fire.' Then he mimed pressing the alarm. '*Oops!*'

Gavin turned, saw Rissa walking down the corridor. Then in a really loud voice: 'Oh, better go, here's your girlfriend!'

And Barney went bright red so fast that Gavin pressed his palms against his cheeks.

'I was right!' the bully exclaimed, feeling the burning heat of Barney's shame. 'There *was* a fire. Right on your face!'

A Tiny, Tiny Moment in Time

'Don't worry too much,' said Rissa stepping off the bus at their stop. 'Your mum's a good person. She's not going to scream at you on your birthday.'

'She might,' said Barney. 'But I just don't want her to go into meltdown. She's going to be so upset with me.'

Rissa thought. 'Well, if you want me to stay with you and explain Miss Whipmire is a nutcase then . . .'

Barney looked at his friend's face. He could see in her eyes that she was genuine. But he didn't want to drag her into this. 'No. It's OK. This is my problem.'

When they were nearly at Barney's house, he and Rissa saw a cat lying on the pavement right in front of his gate. It was just a very normal-looking cat. Not like the silver-haired, one-eyed cat Barney saw most mornings.

No. This one was just your average, run-of-the-mill black cat, with *two* eyes, although one of those eyes – the left – did have a patch of white around it.

'Hello, cat!' Rissa said, and crouched down to stroke it. 'I *so* want a cat.'

'Why don't you get one?' asked Barney.

'Oh, my mum and dad say it might be a bit risky with us living on the river. But I'm, like, *Come on, guys, cats aren't stupid. They can balance on fences so they're hardly likely to slip off a barge.*'

Barney stood there as Rissa carried on stroking the little fellow.

'Wouldn't it be great,' she said, 'just lying down and being stroked by giants all day long, without a care in the world?'

At which point the cat looked towards Barney as if waiting for him to answer.

'Yes, it would.'

'Anyway, I'd better get going, Mister Birthday.' Rissa stood up. She still had over a mile until she was home, but that was OK – Rissa loved walking. 'I'm meant to be helping Dad pick vegetables at his allotment. We're going to put them in a curry. Vegetarian, obviously. But you're welcome to come round if you haven't got anything better to do than sit listening to my dad singing ancient songs very badly.'

Barney thought for a moment. It certainly was tempting, especially as Rissa's parents were about as

nice as parents could get before they tipped off the
edge and became friends.

But he thought of the letter in his bag, which made
him feel an extra weight – far heavier than the paper
and envelope themselves. The weight of dread. 'I'd
better stay in and wait for Mum,' he told his friend.
'I don't want her getting more freaked out than she
already will be.'

'No worries,' said Rissa, smiling warmly. And then
she clapped a hand on Barney's shoulder.

'Listen, Barns, I'm there for you, OK? I know you might get in an incy-wincy bit of trouble tonight, but just think, this is only a tiny, tiny moment in time. Think of the stars. Think of *our* star. The sun. It is billions of years old. And it's going to keep shining whatever happens. Look, in a year's time this will be nothing. In *ten* years' time, when you've got a long beard, you won't even remember it.'

'I won't have a long beard,' said Barney. 'I won't even have a short one.'

'Hey, my *dad's* got a beard. There is *nada* wrong with beards, I'll have you know. Think of all the great, important people in history: Jesus, Emperor Hadrian . . . erm . . . *Father Christmas* – they all had beards.'

'I don't think I'd suit hairy,' said Barney. Then he saw the cat looking up at him. 'No offence.'

Rissa walked away. 'See you tomorrow morning. Same time, same place.'

'Yeah. See you, Rissa, and, thanks – I liked the card.'

'Good. You made me one, so it was the least I could do. And, er, good luck with your mum.'

Barney watched her walk down the street with her mad hair and her long coat and her black boots with the daisies on them. Instead of going back inside, Barney stayed still for a moment.

Same time, same place.

There was something scary about that, Barney thought. About how life was destined to stay the same. Especially when life came with such added ingredients as Gavin Needle and Miss Whipmire.

The cat carried on looking at him, and Barney felt a little bit uneasy so he went inside and read the letter.

Dear Mrs Willow,

I am writing to inform you that your son, Barney, is a disgrace. His behaviour has become increasingly bad over the last few months, his teachers tell me, and now it has reached such terribly despicable levels that I am obliged to write you another letter. And, one way or another, this will be his last.

Today, when he was meant to be in French class, Barney set off the school fire alarm. I saw him do this with my own eyes, and I am sure I don't need to tell you about the obvious and intended disruption this caused.

So it is my duty to tell you that if Barney commits a similar offence again he will be EXPELLED from Blandford High.

Now, as his mother it is your job to make sure you discipline him very firmly to prevent this happening. I would recommend stopping all pocket money, switching off the TV, making sure he reads the right kind of books (very long and boring ones — such as dictionaries) and forcing him to spend lengthy periods in his room thinking about what a terrible boy he has become.

Yours disappointedly,

Miss P. Whipmire
Head Teacher

The Wish

Barney put down the letter and saw his reflection in the old mirror in the hallway.

'I hate being you,' he told it in a whisper.

Then he had a thought, which made him feel happy. He didn't *have* to give his mum the letter. If Miss Whipmire ever did phone to check, it was more than likely his mum would be out. So all he had to do was get rid of the letter.

No letter, no trouble.

Simple.

He'd just throw it in the bin. Yeah, that was what he'd do. But which bin? The one in the kitchen was too risky, and even the one in the garden wasn't fool proof, especially with the amount of things his mum lost in a day and had to go hunting all over for. So he went back outside with his rucksack.

The cat wasn't there now. Barney just kept walking – down the street and round the corner to the bin outside the newsagent's.

He held the letter over the bin. He read it again. Barney knew it was bad to destroy the evidence, but the evidence was wrong.

So he ripped up the letter until it was little pieces of confetti.

On his way back home, tiny white pieces of the letter escaped in the wind, falling around Barney's feet like snow that couldn't melt.

He picked out certain words on the scraps of paper:

```
disgrace
behaviour
Barney
EXPELLED
```

Barney was particularly pleased to see that last piece of paper – the one with EXPELLED on it – end up in a muddy brown puddle.

But, just as he was nearing the corner of Dullard Street, he heard a quiet tinkling sound behind him. Turning, he saw the black and white cat again. It stared up at Barney.

'What do you want, cat?'

The cat, being a cat, didn't tell him – or not in any language Barney could have understood – so he kept on walking. So did the cat.

Then, when Barney reached his street, he saw something that caused his heart to sink and anchor in his stomach. It was his mum's little red car, driving down the road then parking outside the house. Barney looked at his watch.

4.25.

She wasn't due back from the library for over two and a half hours.

He stood still, literally frozen with dread.

She knows.

That's the only explanation.

He imagined Miss Whipmire ringing her at the library and saying, 'Your son has a letter for you. Make sure you get it!'

Then Barney felt something rub against his ankle. He looked down at the cat and remembered what Miss Whipmire had said.

That would be the life, wouldn't it? To be a cat, lying out in the sun, without all those human worries . . .

Barney crouched down behind a hedge. He had no idea why he did this. To avoid his mum, yes. But he knew he'd have to go home some time.

Now, before I go on and tell you what happens next I should point out that Barney really wasn't scared of his mum shouting at him. I mean, she *would* have shouted at him, and that wouldn't have been nice, but the thing Barney dreaded was the bit after.

The bit where his mum would *cry*. Which was also the bit where Barney would feel so bad he'd want to turn into a piece of dust.

Or a cat.

Barney stayed crouching, the cat came close again, and now Barney found himself reaching out a hand to stroke it.

Miss Whipmire's words kept replaying in his head. *To be a cat . . . To be a cat . . .*

'Fancy swapping places?' he asked. He was joking, of course, but a part of the joke was serious. Especially when he said the most important words he had ever spoken in his life:

'I wish I was you.'

The cat stayed looking at him with its green eyes, and Barney suddenly felt a little strange.

Dizzy. As though the street had turned into a merry-go-round. That wasn't the strangest thing, though. The strangest thing was the cat itself.

There was something odd about the patch of white fur around its eye. And Barney realized why – a second ago it had been around the cat's left eye. Now it had switched.

'Don't be stupid,' Barney told himself. 'That's impossible.'

Meanwhile – and Barney couldn't be absolutely sure of this – it *seemed* as though things in the street were changing.

Everything seemed more vivid, brighter, bursting with life. The leaves on the trees became greener, the flowers in the front gardens grew taller and stood prouder, and a plant – a flowerpot on an outside windowsill containing a herb Barney didn't recognize – seemed to visibly shake and tremble as it grew, eventually causing it to fall off and smash on the ground.

'This is not happening,' Barney said. 'This is a dream.'

Barney stood up, or tried to. The street was spinning so fast he toppled back a few steps, knocking himself against a postbox.

'Ow!'

He closed his eyes.

The world became still again.

When he opened his eyes once more, Barney could see the cat trotting quickly away.

'Weird.'

Then he turned to look up his street and saw his mum stepping out of her car to head inside the house.

Behind him, a door opened.

'What's happening out here?'

Barney turned to see an old man staring at him, his face creased with anger as much as age. Barney realized it had been this guy's plant pot that had fallen and smashed on the ground.

'I don't know,' Barney said.

'Don't know? Don't *know*?'

'No. Honestly. I'm sorry.'

'I know your mother. I'll be telling her you go

around knocking people's plants over.'

'It wasn't me. It was no one. It just happened.'

'Plant pots don't fall by themselves – sorry. Not unless there's a hurricane. And I don't feel a hurricane, do you?'

Barney shook his head. 'No, I don't.'

The old man didn't say anything after that. He just looked at Barney, and then at the smashed pot and the earth and the plant on the ground, and sighed a long sigh that seemed to contain a whole lifetime of regret, before going back inside his house.

And that was when Barney knew it was time to go home.

The Infinite Tiredness

A brief wave of tiredness came over Barney as he opened the front door.

His mum was hoovering and didn't look up. Guster came over to greet Barney but unusually his tail wasn't wagging, and his eyes had a gleam of mistrust about them.

Then his mum saw him and switched off the hoover.

'Hello,' Barney said. But he said it like a question. 'Hello?'

His mum just looked at him, without the faintest trace of crossness. 'Oh, hello, sweetheart.'

Sweetheart?

'Why are you back early?' asked Barney, trying not to sound suspicious.

His mum sighed.

This was it! This was the moment she was going to tell him off!

But no.

'I just felt a bit guilty about this morning,' she said.

'What about?'

'Well, it's your birthday, and I didn't really have time for you. So I thought I'd take you somewhere.'

Barney was confused. For a moment he wished he hadn't ripped up the letter. Maybe this was the point he should confess everything. After all, his mum was surely going to find out, and she did seem to be in a particularly good mood. And that was quite rare these days.

'Mum, I—'

'Pizza? Do you fancy going out for a pizza?'

Barney remembered the dream last night. Of being with his dad in a pizza restaurant. 'I . . . er . . .'

'Or a curry?'

'Yeah. A curry sounds good.'

Then his mum gave him a present. It was a book called *How to Improve Your Maths Skills*.

'I know it's not the most exciting present in the world,' said Mrs Willow. (Even though his mum and dad had got divorced, Barney's mum had kept her married name as her maiden name was Rowbottom, and she didn't like that very much because she'd always been called 'Growbottom' as a child.) 'But I just thought it would help you get better marks.'

Barney wanted to explain that the only way he could get better marks was if he moved to a school where there was no Miss Whipmire. But he didn't want to sound ungrateful.

'Oh, thanks.'

And then Barney's mum nearly cried.

'What's the matter?'

She took a deep, pulling-herself-together breath.

'Nothing. You just looked like your . . . Anyway, come on, let's get ready. I'll ring up and book a table for six p.m. I'm quite hungry, aren't you?'

So they went for a meal, and Barney ate the most delicious prawn jalfrezi he had ever tasted. But afterwards he felt weird. The tiredness came back, along with an odd feeling in his bones, as if they were being squeezed. He also felt a bit sick.

'You *do* look pale,' Mrs Willow said, staring at Barney's empty plate. 'I hope it's not the prawns.' She quickly asked for the bill and stood up.

And that was when an infinite tiredness took over Barney and he leaned forward and fell asleep on his dirty plate.

Barney's Dream

You know that expression I just used – '*fell* asleep'? Well, Barney did, but he'd never really understood exactly what it meant. Not until now, as he lay on his plate, falling through layers of treacly blackness. Down and down he fell, watching a shape float above him. A white shape, which at first he thought was a kind of cloud. But he recognized the shape of it, like a blurry number 6, and he realized this was the exact same shape as the patch of white fur around that cat's eye.

And this shape grew and grew until eventually light had taken over the dark, and he was walking through this empty white landscape, to nowhere in particular. It was like walking through the Arctic, except without the cold. Not that it was warm, either. It was absolutely neutral. A place beyond temperature.

But then he heard a voice.

'Barney!'

It was a voice he knew as well as any in the world.

'Barney! I'm over here! This way!'

Barney looked around him but he couldn't see anyone. He strained his eyes, as if to find a word on a blank sheet of paper. It was useless, but he kept trying. He was getting desperate now, because he wanted to see the person the voice belonged to.

He wanted, in short, to see his father.

'Dad! Dad? Where are you?'

'I'm still here, Barney. I'm alive!'

'But *where*? I can't see you.'

'You'll find me. Don't worry!'

'Dad? I can't see you!'

And suddenly Barney felt darkness start to leak onto the white, descending in little moving lashes, like a thousand cat's tails. Still he heard his dad's voice, getting fainter and fainter. 'I'll see you soon,' he said. 'I'll see you soon . . .'

'What?' asked Barney.

Then he felt something shaking his shoulders, and he looked up to see his mum.

'Barney? Are you OK?' his mum asked, examining his pale, jalfrezi-streaked face. 'I think you might need the day off school tomorrow.'

And Barney nodded. 'Yes,' he said. Or tried to.

When he opened his mouth the only sound that came out was a strange release of air.

Like a gasp.

Or a *hiss*.

So he tried again. 'Yes.' And this time his voice was there.

Then, when he got home, he was strangely wide awake and shot upstairs, feeling the need to write something down, as if he almost knew that writing things down was something he might not be able to do in the future.

SOME FACTS ABOUT DAD
by Barney Willow

He snored so loud you could hear it through TWO walls.

He thought he was very good at reading maps but he was actually NOT.

He could smile even when he was sad. He said it came from being a salesman. (He won the *Employee of the Month* award at Blandford Garden Centre for selling the most potted plants.)

His dream was to own his own garden centre.

He liked going on holiday to places that were in the middle of nowhere and which were – ideally – cold and wet. (Mad!)

He liked long walks. (His favourite long walk was in Bluebell Wood.)

He loved cats but Mum never let him have one.

He knew a million facts about plants, and told me quite a lot of them. For instance, he told me that there is a rare plant that grows in the Andes in South America called *Puya raimondii* which doesn't grow a flower until it is 150 years old. Then it dies.

His favourite flowers were simple ones, like daffodils and bluebells. ('Nature's at her best when she's not showing off,' he said.)

He was a good swimmer. Except in backstroke, where he always crashed into the side of the pool.

He had RUBBISH taste in music. He only liked stuff with loud guitars and not much singing, which Mum always said sounded like someone was strangling a cat. (She was right.)

He had big bushy eyebrows that looked like caterpillars.

His favourite food was Mum's apple and blackberry crumble (with custard).

He used to take me to the cinema even though it gave him a headache.

He is not out there. I will not find him. It was just another dream. IT WAS JUST ANOTHER DREAM.

The Hairs

Barney still felt wide awake from his deep nap at the restaurant, and was allowed to stay up late as it was his birthday.

'That was very odd, you falling asleep like that,' his mum commented. 'I think we might need to take you to hospital to get you checked out.'

'I'm all right now. I think I'm feeling better.'

But then, while he sat on the sofa watching TV with his mum, his arms started itching and he began to rub them.

'Barney, don't do that. You'll make them sore,' Mum said, switching from polar bears to a quiz show.

'I can't help it.' He unbuttoned one of his cuffs, rolled up the sleeve and started to scratch the skin directly. 'They're so *itchy*.'

As he scratched he saw one, then two, then *three* thick black hairs on his right arm. They were pure jet-black, way darker than his normal mousy mid-brown hair colour, and were arranged like points in a neat line just below his wrist.

'Mum, look – these hairs.'

'Oh yes, you're turning into a man. Well, now that you're nearly a teenager you'll be starting to get hairy all over the place.'

'But they're weird. They're *black*. I don't have black hair. And they weren't there yesterday. They weren't even there this afternoon. I don't want to turn into a man *that* quickly.'

She wasn't listening. She was too busy looking at his forehead.

'What is it?' Barney asked her.

'Oh dear, I'll just get the tweezers,' she said, before disappearing up to her bedroom.

Meanwhile, Barney went to look in the hallway mirror to see what the matter was.

There, right in the middle of his forehead, was another thick black hair.

'Right,' his mum said, running back down the stairs. 'I've got the tweezers. Let's pluck it out. Stand under the light so I can get a good look at it.'

Barney did as she instructed, staring up at the bulb, which shone little white whiskers of light. A part of him quite enjoyed his mum giving him so much attention. But another part of him was worried.

'Mum, what's happening to me?'

'Nothing's *happening*,' she reassured him. 'Bodies are strange things. You can get hairs anywhere.'

'But I feel itchy as well. My arms, and my legs.'

'Well, don't scratch right now,' she said. 'Stay still and we'll get this out.'

Barney stayed still even though his skin felt like it was covered with a hundred invisible mosquito bites.

'Right,' his mum said. 'This might hurt just a little bit.'

She pressed the tweezers together, jamming the hair between the ends. Then she started to pull. And pull.

And *pull*.

She had one hand pressed onto his head and the other was trying to tug out the hair. Barney winced, his eyes watering from the pain as the hair was pulled and tugged and yanked.

'How weird,' she mused. 'It just won't come out.'

A horrible image flashed into Barney's mind. He imagined walking into school and Gavin making even more jokes about him than normal. *Hey, look at the werewolf!* Or something equally hilarious.

Then his mum went and got the cream she used on her upper lip to stop her getting a moustache, but that didn't do anything except add a red circle around the black hair – just in case it wasn't noticeable enough already.

Barney wanted to tell her that this needed to be sorted out, but he felt another wave of overwhelming tiredness. This time, though, he managed not to fall asleep right there. He just yawned a 'Goodnight' and a 'Better go up' to his mum, and had a vague thought that he should confess about the letter, but he couldn't. He didn't have the courage. Or the *energy*.

Instead he promised to wash his face and brush his teeth, and climbed upstairs in a sleepy trance. Then he went to bed (*without* washing his face or brushing his teeth – or even closing his curtains), collapsing on his mattress and pulling the duvet over him before falling into the deepest, darkest sleep of his life.

Waking Up

Before he even opened his eyes for the day to begin, Barney knew something was wrong.

His mouth felt like a desert. His heart was racing fast but gently, like a drum roll at low volume. But that wasn't all. His whole body felt different. Warmer, for one thing, but also more hunched in, like a closed fist that couldn't open.

He could feel a softness on top of him. A big, heavy *softness*. When he opened his eyes it made no difference, because it was still totally dark. Quickly, though, he could see patterns in front and around him, as if he had suddenly developed night vision.

Long, black, teardrop-shaped shadows stood out against grey.

I'm in a cave.

A very soft, low – and particularly warm – cave.

As he became more alert he realized this was ridiculous. He decided he must be under his own duvet. But how could it have grown so *big*?

Barney tried to get to his feet but couldn't, or at least not in the way he normally got to his feet. He was standing up, and yet his back was still pressed against the soft, warm gigantic cave of a duvet.

He moved forward, but his arms and legs weren't working like they normally did. Something was wrong with his coordination. And where were his knees? What had happened to them? It was as though his skeleton was a jigsaw puzzle that had been mixed up overnight. Things that should have bent didn't. Things that shouldn't have did. And some pieces of his bone-jigsaw were entirely new. Most notably, he could feel something trailing behind his back. Something that he could move in various ways as if it was made of ten elbows joined together.

Mum, he said, or tried to. And then, pointlessly: *Dad*. But he couldn't make words, just noises.

Trapped as he was in this strange new body, he started to panic. Barney urgently wanted to get out of the darkness, and the only way he could think of doing that was to crawl from under it. So he did. Shuffling forward on his new limbs, with his head low and his legs close to the spongy floor, he pushed his way through.

And then he was there, out in the cold light of morning.

He looked down to see a great vastness that at first seemed like an ocean. The length of the drop was at least three times his height so it took a moment to realize that the great blue vastness he was looking down at was his own carpet.

This was his bed.

This was his room.

But everything had grown beyond all possibility. The wardrobe was the size of a house. The bedside lamp peered down at him like some strange armless robot. The door was miles away. And the school uniform which hung over his chair belonged to a giant.

Next he saw something which made even less sense.

His hands, or his feet – he couldn't tell which – were entirely covered with hair. And they were fingerless. Toeless. He turned his head to see what he had only felt so far. A tail. Curled into a quivering kind of question mark, as though the rest of his body was a query wanting an answer.

It was impossible.

He was still Barney. His 'Barney-ness' was still there in his head, his mind still the same bulging suitcase of memories and emotions. But at the same time he already knew he wasn't him at all. He was something else. Something so impossible that he thought this *had* to be a dream, like the one he'd had about his father.

He blinked, and then blinked some more.

No. There was no doubt about it.

He was awake.

Indeed, he was as awake as he had ever been. So, to his horror, he had to believe what his eyes were telling him, and what the black hair and the tail and the paws were telling him. And what they were telling him was this: he may have gone to bed human, but he had woken up unquestionably, unmistakably, unimaginably *cat*.

The Jump

Noises.

His mother taking an item of cutlery from a kitchen drawer. Something he wouldn't normally have been able to hear from up here. Now it was as sharp as if he was in the room with her.

She was feeding Guster. He heard the spoon tap three times against the ceramic bowl, shaking off the dog food.

Mum! Barney shouted. Except he didn't, obviously, as his mouth didn't work any more. It was a cat's mouth, dry, which could conjure nothing more than the feeblest miaow.

Then his whiskers curled (cat-magic trick number six, as you'll remember) and tingled with the knowledge of imminent danger; a danger that soon made every one of the hundred thousand new hairs on his body stand on end.

Guster.

Within five seconds of the food reaching his bowl

64

Guster would have gobbled his breakfast. Then he would do one of two things. Either he'd fall asleep in his basket or – most likely – he'd trot quickly into the bedroom to lick Barney's face. Only today he wouldn't be able to find *Barney's* face. He'd find a *cat's* face. And Barney knew that Guster was to cats what an oven was to ice cream.

A memory flashed in his mind: Guster chasing after a Siamese cat in the park. The cat had disappeared out of view before Guster got the chance to do anything, but that was only because it had been a super-fast cat, disappearing as if by magic in a second or two.

At the time, as Barney had jogged after Guster, it had seemed quite amusing. But now he was the cat he couldn't see the funny side.

He looked down at the carpet.

Jump. You have to jump.

If you don't get out of here, Guster will kill you.

And there it was.

The rising, deadly thunder as the spaniel galloped up the stairs.

Jump! Barney told himself one last time.

He closed his eyes. Saw his dad's face at the side of a swimming pool, long ago, encouraging Barney to jump from the diving board. *You can do it, Barney.* He heard the pounding of heavy paws against carpet as the potential cat-killer ran up the stairs.

You have to do this. On three.

One, two—

In the self-imposed darkness Barney dropped down into the air, smooth as water pouring from a glass.

But he landed hard and heavy, his peculiar new head hitting the carpet. Things blurred, then sharpened back into shape. *No time to think.* Guster was upstairs now, his panting breath getting closer.

Barney ran. He didn't know how, being so rearranged, but he managed it quite easily. Hid in the corner of the room, nothing but his fear for company, while Guster nudged the giant door open with his nose.

The door swung back giving Barney something to hide behind as he tried to ignore the voice of his own doubts, telling him he was about to die.

Guster jumped on the bed, sniffing traces of boy, traces of cat, traces of whatever was in between. Then, creating what felt to Barney like a brief earthquake, he jumped off the bed.

This is not happening, Barney told himself. *I am not a cat. I am a human being. I am a boy. A twelve-year-old boy. Everything will be—*

A wet canine nose peered round the door; two black nostrils, like eyes on a monstrous face. The nose waited a moment, working something out. And then the nose nudged the door backwards, and suddenly Guster's whole face was there, with its caramel-brown and white fur and bright eyes, high above Barney. He seemed ten times bigger than normal. A King Charles *monster*.

Then the most incredible thing of all. A voice. A pompous, almost regal voice came from Guster. 'Oh my goodness! One is simply *lost* for words! A horrible feline. In my house. *My* house!'

'No, it's me,' Barney tried, and realized he was understood – by Guster, at least. 'It's Barney. Guster, honestly, you have to believe me. I don't know what's going on. I just . . . in the night something must have . . .'

'What are you doing here? What is your intention? Speak! Speak, I beseech you!'

There was a demented madness in Guster's eyes. He looked capable of anything.

'It's me!'

'Confine your tongue!' Guster barked crossly. 'Do you know who you're talking to? I am a King Charles spaniel. My ancestors were there to witness the restoration of the King of England. They helped make this country what it is today. And, like all my noble breed, I have a strong set of principles that I live by religiously. Of the utmost importance is this – never let an uninvited *feline* into your house. If such a thing should happen, one has no choice but to kill said feline. So, you furry vagabond, I suggest you prepare to die.'

'Oh, Guster, what on earth is the matter? Stop barking!' This was Barney's mother, calling from downstairs. 'I've got a headache.'

Mum! Barney tried to shout. *Mum! Mum!*

Three pathetic miaows, not even worthy of speech marks.

Guster growled, showed teeth. Teeth he planned to use.

'Guster, listen,' Barney said, and was thankful at least that Guster could hear him. 'It's me – Barney. Ask me anything you want. Something only I would know and—'

The dog moved closer, gnashing his jaws. Barney backed into the wall. Normally, as a human, nothing in the world can look as cute and innocent as a King Charles spaniel. But Barney was now seeing things from a whole new angle.

'You treacherous, lowly moggy!'

'Guster! Honestly, I'm Barney. It was my birthday yesterday. My dad is missing, presumed dead. My dad – you know, the one who chose you from that rescue centre.'

Guster seemed suddenly furious at the mention

of this. '*Rescue centre?* What a blot on my honour. How *dare* you? I must tell you again – I am a King Charles spaniel. My ancestors lived in the royal court of King Charles the Second, enjoying such privileges as no dog has ever known. Rescue centre! What an insult.'

Barney didn't know what else to say. 'But it's true. Your last owners, they didn't want you any more. So we saved you. *Dad* saved you.'

Guster paused. He seemed to be thinking about something. For a moment Barney thought his words might have got through. That he might have found an ally in Guster. But no.

'*Liar-gggh!*' Guster growled.

And then his jaws opened and came speeding towards Barney's new head.

I'm going to die, I'm going to die, I'm going to—

Barney closed his eyes and waited for his head to be bitten off, but it didn't happen.

Giant teeth were only a thin whisker from Barney when suddenly the dog was yanked high away. Mrs Willow had grabbed him by the collar just in time, saving Barney's life.

Barney opened his eyes to see a giant lady towering above him.

And his mum saw him. Except she didn't know who she was seeing, of course.

'Oh my God,' she said. 'A cat! Barney, could you please tell me what a *cat* is doing in your room? Barney? Barney . . . ? *Barney?*'

She was looking at the empty bed, wondering where her son was. Barney could see the worry in her distant face, setting in like bad weather.

'Barney, are you in the bathroom?' she called. 'Are you still having trouble with that hair?'

No, Barney said. *No, I'm here. I'm the cat. It's me. Mum, please, listen. Mum!*

He looked up at her. It was like trying to convince a cathedral.

'You trespassing *liar*,' snapped Guster. 'Please, Mrs Willow, let me deal with this vagabond.'

'Come on, Guster.' Mum pulled the dog away. She went and shut him in Barney's father's old office, which was now the spare room. 'Now, you stay there,' Barney heard her say. 'And no scratching at the door.'

A moment later she was back. She crouched down, and he felt her hand underneath his stomach then – *whoosh* – he was pulled high into the air. He tried to hold onto her dressing gown, and his claws appeared and tucked themselves into the fabric.

'Don't do that, you naughty thing,' said his mother. 'Now, where's Barney? Barney?! Where are you? I really haven't got time for this!'

I'm here! You're carrying me!

She hauled Barney around the house, her grip getting tighter with every new room she couldn't find her son in.

Eventually Mrs Willow opened the front door, detached Barney from her dressing gown and dropped him to the ground, out in the frosty February air.

Mum! he cried. *Mum! Don't worry! I'm—*

The giant door closed with a heavy thud and he was left there.

Cold.

Confused.

And infinitely alone.

The No-Hoper

Barney waited on the porch for a while, expecting his mother to realize he wasn't anywhere in the house and hoping she'd make the connection. But the door didn't open. It just stayed there, a gigantic piece of unfriendly wood, which Barney's dad had painted three years ago when he still lived there.

The usually quiet street felt full of a hundred noises – twittering birds, distant traffic, crisp packets scraping concrete as they travelled with the breeze.

Another noise. Rustling, coming from the little juniper bush in the garden. Two green cat's eyes staring at him.

'Hello?'

'Who are you?' the cat asked tenderly, in a voice as soothing as hot cocoa. 'I've never seen you before.'

She stepped out of the bush. She was a sleek, chocolate-brown cat that Barney vaguely recognized as belonging to Sheila, the new arrival at number 33.

'Yes, you have,' Barney said as this other cat came

and rubbed her head against the side of his face. 'I'm the boy who lives here. In this house. It's just . . . I've changed . . . and I don't know why.'

'Oh,' she said, and then she said it again (only this time in italics). '*Oh.* Oh, you poor thing. You poor little sardine. You're one of *them*.'

'One of who? Wait . . . does this happen to other people too?'

'Oh yes. It does. I'm Mocha, by the way, and I'm very pleased to meet you.' She purred, but then her mood switched at cat-speed and the purring stopped. Mocha started to look anxious.

Barney, though, needed answers. 'Look, do you know why I'm like this? Do you know how I can change back? Could you help me?'

Mocha was looking past Barney now to the street. Her tail twitched, and her whiskers were curling slightly. She was sensing something. 'I think, sweetie, we're being watched.'

'Watched? By who?'

'By swipers, most probably.'

'Swipers? What are they?'

Mocha turned to Barney and gave a rushed explanation, her soothing hot-chocolate voice now fast and nervous, like his mum's after too much coffee.

'There are three types of cats,' she said, then named them. 'There are swipers, who are tough street cats, and who you need to be scared of. Then there are firesides, like me, who have owners and who generally prefer staying at home. We aren't scary, as a rule, not unless you try and bathe us. Well, apart from the . . .' She hesitated, as if frightened to finish her sentence. 'Apart from the Terrorcat.'

'The Terrorcat? Who's that?'

Mocha came closer, to whisper. 'I hope you never find out.'

'Why? What makes him so scary?'

'He was just a normal cat once, but then he changed, just as a night follows a sunset,' Mocha said with a shudder. 'He developed powers, dark and evil powers, and became something else. He looked the same. But he was very, very different . . . '

'What made him change?'

But Barney wasn't going to get an answer on this one. You see, Mocha had just spotted something: a fat, thuggish ginger moggy on the other side of the street, lying under a parked car, staring straight at them. Or rather, straight at Barney.

'Is that the Terrorcat?'

'No, my dear. You would know about it if that was

the Terrorcat. That's Pumpkin. A swiper. He's stupid. But violent. And he's got a lot of equally stupid, equally violent friends.'

'Why's he watching me?'

'I don't know,' she said, and suddenly seemed less keen to be friends. 'Now, I'd love to hang around, truthfully, but my owner – Sheila – she's going on holiday today and I'm going to the cattery, and I wouldn't miss it for the world.'

'I thought cats hated catteries.'

'Not this one. It's lovely.'

The cat started to trot away down the side of the house. 'But wait!' Barney called after her. 'What about the third type of cat? You only mentioned two.'

Mocha stopped, tail-twitched, turned. 'That's your type. Former humans trapped in cat bodies.'

'What are we called?' Barney said, stalling for time and wanting Mocha to stay with him as long as she possibly could.

'The no-hopers,' Mocha told him sadly. 'Because it's true. You really have no hope.'

Best Friend(ly Giant)

Barney looked around nervously. Saw the ginger moggy still staring at him. Perhaps he should have followed Mocha. But, no. He wanted to stay here in the hope of convincing his mum who he was, even if it meant being at the mercy of a swiper.

The fat ginger cat started to walk out from under the car. He beckoned down the street with his tail, and soon there were other cats there too. Street cats of varying shapes and furs prowling menacingly towards him.

'Right, lads, this is the boy,' said Pumpkin. 'Do yer worst on 'im.'

The cats got closer and closer.

'Wait,' said Barney. 'Please, I don't want any trouble.'

'Well, that's all we's be wantin', see,' Pumpkin sneered. 'That's all we about, innit, fellas? Trouble. And the causing thereof. And, besides, we be 'avin' our orders.'

'Who's ordered you?' Barney asked, panicking as three more swipers headed up the path. One, an evil-looking cat with oversized ears, hissed in Barney's face. 'Prepare to die!'

Barney had no idea how he would prepare for his death so thought he'd better try and avoid it for a while. He backed away, heading down the side of the house. 'Mocha? Are you still there? I might actually need some help here.'

But if Mocha could hear him, she certainly wasn't saying.

'Now, swipers,' said the ginger moggy. 'Let's be showin' what we're made of.'

'What *he's* made of, you mean,' laughed big-ears, her claws at the ready.

'Wotchit, Lyka. I do the jokes round here.'

Barney tried to run away but he was faced with a giant compost heap blocking his path. He tried to climb over it but his feet kept sinking into the mush of leaves and earth and weeds, some of which had probably been thrown there by his dad over two years ago. There were now five cats down the passageway, and they all had their hair raised and their claws out, ready to pounce.

And I can assure you they would have pounced if

they hadn't heard something behind them.

Or rather, some*one*. Humming tunefully to themselves as they walked along the path.

'Pumpkin, what shall we do?' asked Lyka in her evil cat hiss.

'We can't be doin' no murder with 'oomans round. You's know the rules.' So, on Pumpkin's orders, the street cats fled, running over the compost heap and over Barney, their sharp claws scratching him as they went.

'Don't worry,' said Pumpkin, before disappearing across the top of the heap. 'We be seein' you shortly.'

Barney felt sick. His cat nostrils could pick up smells a human nose would miss, and there seemed to be a million different queasy odours coming from the compost heap which, mixed with his fear, was really too much to bear.

Somehow he pulled himself together enough to leave the narrow passageway and run back round to the front of his house.

He saw a pair of boots he recognized. Black boots with a daisy painted on the ankles, now sidestepping a window-cleaner's ladder and then walking up the path.

It was Rissa.

Of *course* it was Rissa. For her and for everyone

else, this was a totally normal Wednesday morning at – well, Barney worked out it must have been about quarter past eight if Rissa was on time.

Rissa, he called. *Rissa!*

Even when he tried to shout her name as loud as he could, all that came out was a faint, breathless miaow. Watching her giant feet take T. rex strides up his path he felt a heavy sadness in his stomach. He crawl-walked towards her and nudged his head against her ankles.

She stopped and looked down. Slowly her face broadened into a smile.

Rissa, Barney kept on saying, even though he was beginning to realize it was pointless. *It's me, Barney. Please understand me . . . please understand me . . .*

His friend kept smiling, but it was that empty smile you give to animals, not humans.

'Hey! Hello, cat,' she said.

She crouched down and stroked the top of Barney's head. Her hand seemed massive, *was* massive, like the hand of some monster in a 3D movie that had actually managed to break through the fourth dimension.

I'm not a cat, he said, feeling a weird itch in his ear. *I'm your best friend.*

'Where do you live?' She asked him this the way people ask animals questions, without expecting an

answer, but he gave her one anyway.

You know where I live. I live at seventeen Dullard Street. That's right here. This very house. Barney panicked, the memory of Pumpkin and the swipers burning like the scratches on his back. *Please, you've got to help me. It's dangerous out here.*

Rissa kept smiling, then stroked her best friend under his chin, which he found quite annoying. Not that it was her fault, or anything. How could she know who the cat she was stroking really was? How could anyone know?

'Well, gotta go,' she told him. 'You're lucky. You're a cat. You don't have to go to school.'

No. No. I am not lucky. I am deeply unlucky. Rissa, please, it's me.

She stood up. She hummed happy human tunes, then rang the doorbell.

Barney stayed still for a moment.

Then he realized. She was calling at his house. The house he wasn't in, and his mum was going to answer and say he wasn't there, and Barney would be able to miaow at them like crazy and maybe – just *maybe* – they would understand.

D. I. E.

Barney had felt a bit like this before, in the old days before his parents divorced. Obviously he'd never actually *been* a cat, but he'd felt that feeling of not having a voice. Or rather, not having a voice that anyone properly listened to.

You see, Barney's mum and dad used to have lots of arguments. They'd row about almost anything. They'd row every time they drove in a car together. They'd row about his dad leaving old milk in the fridge when it had gone sour. About whose turn it was to walk Guster last thing at night.

And, after a while, there were no spaces between the rows.

Barney's mum and dad had become trapped in a never-ending argument, and no matter how many times Barney told them to stop, or got them to promise they'd never do it again, they always did do it again.

And it was *horrible*.

When he was in bed Barney used to put his hands

over his ears and close his eyes tight shut, trying to cancel out the shouting. 'Be quiet,' he used to whisper. 'Please, just be quiet.'

But even though he hated his mum and dad getting cross with each other, he hated it even more when they told him they were getting a divorce. When he was younger he didn't really know what 'divorce' meant, although he knew it wasn't good. How could a word with the letters 'd', 'i' and 'e' in it – in that order – mean something nice?

'Dad's not going to live with us any more,' his mum had said.

'What? Why?'

'Because we think you will be happier – and everyone will be happier – if me and your dad live apart.'

'So, you're splitting up because of me?'

'No, Barney, of course not,' his mum said.

'Well, good. Because I want you to stay together. Why can't you both stop arguing? It can't be that hard. At school we learned about Carthusian monks who don't speak for *years*. Why don't you just *not speak*? Then you *couldn't* argue.'

But Barney couldn't convince her. Or his dad, for that matter, who put his hand on Barney's shoulder and said, 'Barney, sometimes what seems like a bad thing is really the best thing.'

'But I won't ever see you.'

'You'll see me on Saturdays. We'll have fun together.'

Barney wasn't impressed. He already had fun on Saturdays. It was Sundays, Mondays, Tuesdays, Wednesdays, Thursdays and Fridays that needed improving. And having a Dad-less house certainly didn't make them any better. In fact, Barney found himself actually *wanting* to hear his mum and dad have an argument, because it would have been better than hearing his mum on her own, crying.

He spent nearly a year like this.

Saturdays with his dad trying too hard to be Mr Fun-Father, going to zoos and theme parks and football matches, which he would never have taken Barney to before.

'You've had fun, haven't you?' his dad always said at the end of each Saturday.

'Yes,' Barney would say, and he'd sometimes mean it, but it was never enough fun to balance out six days of non-fun.

The Barney-Who-Wasn't-Barney

As Barney waited by Rissa's ankles she looked down at him, smiling that same blank smile. *What could he do to prove it was him?*

'Are you still there?' she said.

He could feel a strange vibration inside him, a weird warm mumbling. And then he realized he was *purring*. But he wasn't happy. He was anything but. Yet there it was, a purr that now seemed as loud as a drill. Because purring – that great mystery which has baffled biologists through the ages ('Check the larynx!' 'No, it's not coming from there!') – isn't anything to do with happiness. It's to do with magic. And the sound of purring is the sound of magic itself. Or, rather, the sound of magic capabilities being made.

The door opened and his mother was standing there. He expected her to look pale and worried. After all, she must have known by now that her son was missing. But she didn't look worried at all. In fact, she was smiling.

'Hello, Rissa,' she said. 'How are you?'

'Oh, I'm fine, thanks, Mrs Willow. Is Barney ready?'

This was it.

This was the moment they would realize something was majorly wrong.

Barney waited for his mother to say she hadn't seen him all morning, but it didn't happen. Her smile stayed exactly in place.

But if his mum's behaviour was weird, what she said was even worse.

'Yes,' she said. 'He's just coming. *Barney! Barney! Rissa's here!*'

This didn't make sense.

Barney wasn't coming.

He couldn't be coming.

He was standing out on the pavement.

Yet only moments later, Barney saw someone walking through the darkness of the hallway.

Someone in Barney's uniform.

And now he was there, standing with the sunlight revealing his face.

A twelve-year-old boy's face.

Freckled.

With wavy hair and slightly sticking-out ears.

Barney knew the face.

It was the face he saw in the mirror every single day.

His face. On his body. In his school uniform.

And this Barney-Who-Wasn't-Barney stared down at the Barney-Who-*Was*-Barney and gave him a quiet look which said:

I know.

I know you are me and I am you.

This is what you wanted.

'Hi, Barns,' Rissa said.

The other Barney silently left the house and started walking up the road, with Rissa, a little confused, following behind.

Barney – the *real* Barney – didn't know what to do. So, for a few long moments, he did nothing. Then the door closed, and the sound of it thudding shut brought Barney to his senses.

And that is when he decided to follow Rissa and his other self up the street.

'The sky was amazing last night,' Rissa was saying. 'I could see Ursa Major *and* Ursa Minor.'

The Barney-Who-Wasn't-Barney looked baffled.

'So what did your mum say about the letter?'

She got no answer.

'Barney? Are you *OK*? You seem, I don't know,

a bit blank. Is this about Miss Whipmire?'

Then it happened.

The Barney-Who-Wasn't-Barney started running – sprinting, in fact. He ran to the top of the street, then turned right onto Marlowe Road.

'Barney!' shouted Rissa. 'What are you *doing*? Was it because I mentioned Miss Whipmire?'

The Barney-Who-Wasn't-Barney said nothing, just kept running, and so Barney ran after him as fast as his little legs could take him.

Cat Pancake

Here's some advice:

If you ever become a cat – and it's more likely than you might imagine (there's about a one in 5,000 chance, according to the latest estimates) – don't think about things too much.

What I mean is, don't think, *How can I purr?* because then you won't purr. And certainly – *certainly* – don't think, *How do cats run?* because then you'll struggle. Just as Barney struggled, running along Marlowe Road, trying to find the right paw rhythm – front left, back right, front right, back left – trying to stop his head from hitting the pavement.

And all the time he was watching himself – his body, his hair, his school bag – get further and further away from him. By the time Barney had stopped wondering, *How do cats run?* and actually ran, cat-style, it was too late.

The Barney-Who-Wasn't-Barney had disappeared behind the crowd of school kids at the bus stop. A crowd that included Gavin Needle.

'Oi, Willow!' he was shouting at the boy he thought was Barney. 'Where are you going, you freak?'

Then Gavin stopped, looked down at Barney. The real one. The furry, four-legged version.

'Isn't that—?' said another voice. One of Gavin's cronies.

Barney didn't have time to run away, because suddenly there was a massive knock to his stomach, as if a rowing boat had swung into him. But it wasn't a boat. It was a *boot*. Gavin's boot. And Barney heard cruel laughter as he flew into the air, landing on the road.

Barney froze. A car was speeding towards him. But the only part of Barney that moved were his claws, clinging to the tarmac as the car drove directly over him, its tyres missing him by a whisker.

And then Gavin said something to Barney. Something like, 'What are you doing here?' He might have added a swear word somewhere too, but Barney wasn't listening properly. He was too busy looking to see where his clone had got to, but he couldn't see him. There were traffic lights and crossroads, but it was impossible to know which way this other Barney would have gone.

Straight on, into town? Left down Coleridge Road, the road which the bus took to school? Or right, heading towards the park along Friary Road?

He had no idea.

Then another voice from the pavement. Rissa, breathing heavily: 'Watch out!'

She had run after the Barney-Who-Wasn't-Barney, and now she was at the bus stop with all the others.

Barney turned.

The school bus was heading straight for him, pulling in at the side of the road, its two left tyres right on track to kill him.

The driver hadn't seen him. Because he was too

busy concentrating on his breakfast. He was eating a chocolate bar, as he did every morning.

Cat pancake.

Barney froze, petrified. The noise of the bus was louder than anything he'd ever known.

I'm going to die.

And he really did believe that would be his final thought.

But it wasn't.

Because he was still thinking – mainly about the human hand under his stomach, sweeping him fast into the air – as the side of the bus slid past his face.

That was too close.

For a moment Barney wondered whose hand it was, but then he realized he could feel the cool metal of Rissa's rings and, sure enough, he heard her voice in his ear.

'What are you doing, cat? You were nearly killed.'

She pulled him off her shoulder, looked him straight in the eye.

I'm not a cat, he tried again. *Rissa, I'm Barney.*

This time, just for a second, Barney thought she understood. A glimmer of recognition shone in her eyes. But the glimmer disappeared, like the sun behind a cloud, and she placed Barney down on the pavement.

'Don't go on the road. It's very, very dangerous,' she said. 'Buses and cats don't get on very well. In fact, they're pretty much incompatible. Remember that.'

Gavin kicked me onto the road. I couldn't help it.

She stood up, followed the other Blandford High pupils onto the bus.

Wait.

Barney tried to think. There was no way he was going to catch up with the Barney-Who-Wasn't-Barney. And there was no point going home to a closed door. Even if the door wasn't closed, his mum would just throw him out again. Even if she didn't, Guster would still try to kill him.

Which left—

Rissa.

She was his best hope right now. After all, she'd just saved his life.

So, without thinking much more about it, he padded towards the bus, hid behind the last pair of human legs – Rissa's – and jumped on board.

The Bus

Barney got the school bus every day, so he knew that people normally sat in the same seats.

The twins, Petra and Petula Primm (every teacher's favourites), always sat on the front seat. Gavin Needle and his friends always took over the back two rows.

And Rissa and Barney always sat together, three seats behind Petra and Petula Primm, but on the other side of the aisle, opposite the Blub (who wasn't really called the Blub, he was called Oscar Williams, but that's what Miss Whipmire called him – because he was very fat, and because he had the understandable tendency to cry when slapped in the face by bullies).

So Barney knew where he was going as he kept close behind his friend's heels.

The trouble was the bus driver had finished his chocolate bar now and was paying more attention. And the driver was *sure* he'd seen something sneak onto the bus behind that strange, tall girl with the crazy hair (which is how he thought of Rissa).

He looked in the large round mirror that reflected all his passengers but couldn't see anything. Neither could anyone else. Not even Petula Primm, who had felt something soft and hairy slide against her leg but was so busy talking in excited and secret tones to her sister about a recent trip to their aunt's that she hardly noticed.

Not even Rissa noticed as she was too busy wondering why 'Barney' had run away from her, and away from the bus to school too. What was going on? First the silent treatment, then this.

Maybe he was just worried about Miss Whipmire.

Or maybe he was just missing his dad.

Or maybe he'd become totally insane overnight.

Rissa didn't own a mobile, so she asked to borrow Oscar's and called Barney's mother. After a few rings the answering machine clicked on.

'Hello, Mrs Willow. It's me, Rissa . . .'

Barney was listening from under her seat, struggling to keep his balance as the bus turned corners, and feeling that itchiness in his ear again.

'. . . Look, Mrs Willow, I don't want to get Barney into trouble, or anything. I'm just a bit worried about him . . .'

It was at this point that Gavin shouted from the back seat.

'Mr Bus Driver! Mr Bus Driver!' he called in a pretend goody-goody voice. 'There's a girl using her phone on the bus!'

The next thing Barney knew the bus had pulled to a stop, sending him hurtling forward into Rissa's legs.

Her face appeared in front of him, upside down. '*You!*'

The driver tapped her on the shoulder.

'Now, I'm sure you know the rules about phones on the school bus, young lady!'

'Yes,' said Rissa. 'I do. But this is actually quite important. My friend has just run away.'

The bus driver sneered. 'Not surprised, with hair like that.'

Rissa heard the laughter behind her but wasn't going to back down. 'Look, it's important.'

'Sorry. Rules is rules. Using phones on school buses leads to mugging. That's a known fact.'

'Well, eating chocolate while driving causes traffic accidents,' said Rissa. 'That's *also* a known fact. You nearly ran over a cat before. And, anyway, I never normally use mobile phones. I prefer talking to faces. But this is an emergency.'

''Snot even her phone,' said Oscar.

'Shut up, Blub,' jeered Gavin from the back seat.

The driver wasn't listening to Gavin or Oscar. He was thinking about what Rissa said, and remembering what he might just have seen stepping onto the bus.

'*A cat?*'

Barney's tail was rising with fear as cats' tails do. And Rissa was quick to see it. She knew that if the bus driver saw it, the cat would be thrown off right here, miles from home, so she moved her leg to hide it.

'I'm . . . I'm sorry,' Rissa said, changing her tune. 'For using the phone on the bus. I won't do it again.'

It worked.

The driver gave the phone back to Oscar with a warning to them both, and then returned to his seat.

'Sorry, Oscar,' Rissa said.

''S all right,' Oscar replied.

Barney said thank you to his best friend the only way he could, by nuzzling his head against her ankles.

Cat On The Run

Rissa got Barney off the bus, hiding him inside her coat where he could hear the beating of her heart. Then, when all the others had disappeared through the school gates, she took Barney out into the cool air that he could feel tingling his whiskers.

'Now,' she said. 'Why don't you have a collar?'

Rissa was clearly wondering what to do. Barney realized this. In fact, for a brief moment he could see her thoughts as clearly as if they were fish in a pond. She was wondering if she should borrow someone else's phone and call the RSPCA. That was no good. That would mean being locked in a cage with no chance of proving to anyone who he really was.

Then Barney had a plan. If he ran ahead of Rissa, he could enter the school and get to his classroom, then he could run to his chair.

Why would a cat run through a school to jump on Barney's empty chair unless it *was* Barney?

OK, there were probably other reasons, but this

was as good a plan as he had so he pushed his front paws against Rissa and launched himself into the air. He fell, suddenly realizing he wasn't anywhere near Rissa-height any more and that he had a very long way to drop. He winced, expecting to crash-land painfully, but it didn't happen. In fact, to Barney's astonishment, he fell fluidly through the air and landed with ease on all four paws. And he had to admit it felt pretty good, moving like a cat.

But, as Barney started to run, he saw another cat was watching him suspiciously from the other side of the road. A ginger moggy, licking its front paws and carefully studying him. *Pumpkin!* The shock caused Barney to hesitate.

Rissa's hand was on his back, ready to scoop him up again, so he ran as fast as he could through the open gates and towards the doors of the vast modern school building.

It had always been big, but now it was infinite. Barney couldn't see an end to it, whichever way he looked. Just windows and concrete, windows and concrete, windows and concrete . . .

'Cat! Come here, cat!' Rissa was shouting behind him, getting closer.

Good, thought Barney, encouraged his plan was

working so far, and actually enjoying the sensation of running in his cat body.

Ahead was a Year Thirteen whom Barney recognized – a scruffy boy with lots of spots who always seemed friendly. He was trying to tuck in his shirt as he pushed his way through the two doors that led onto the main school corridor.

The doors closed slowly, so Barney had time to slip inside.

The Year Thirteen noticed Barney run past his ankles. 'Oh, a cat,' he said sleepily as if it was a completely normal thing to see animals running along the school corridor at a quarter to nine in the morning.

Barney could hear Rissa's footsteps on the polished, sickly scented floor but kept going, as determined as if he were taking part in the Cat Olympics. Past reception, Miss Whipmire's office, the staff room, weaving through legs of early pupils wandering the corridors.

'What was that?' said one.

'What?' said another.

'Looked like a . . . *cat*.'

Barney skidded into a left turn, darted past the empty science labs, turned one final corner, and he was

nearly where he wanted to be, with Rissa's footsteps in fast pursuit.

Then he was there. 7R's classroom. The door was open and Mrs Lavender, the nicest teacher in the whole school, was already inside. She was leaning over her desk, putting big red ticks and writing *Very good* next to someone's homework.

A few pupils were already in the room, sitting at their desks, chatting. Barney could see from their feet that Gavin wasn't there yet. That was good. What wasn't good was that some of the other kids had noticed him.

'Look,' said Lottie Lewis, chewing gum. 'It's a cat.'

'OMG!' said Lottie's best friend, Aaliyah. 'How *cute* is that?'

Lottie – who was probably the prettiest and most popular girl in school – leaned down and stroked Barney's back.

'You're *gorgeous*,' she said, picking Barney off the floor.

Great, he thought. *The first time Lottie Lewis has ever noticed me and I'm a cat.*

Rissa was in the room now, out of breath. 'That cat got on the bus,' she explained. 'It's miles from home.'

This wasn't good. She still thought he was a cat,

and now Mrs Lavender had seen what was going on. 'Oh goodness me. Oh my goodness. Goodness! Whose is that? Is that yours, Lottie?'

'No. I just found it.'

Rissa explained again about the cat being found near the bus stop, and Barney was watching Lottie's face and her giant eyelashes like the petals of an exotic plant. She wasn't concentrating, so he wriggled free, over her arm, and jumped onto her desk across Aaliyah's.

Then he leaped down onto the floor and ran to his chair. He prepared himself for the pounce but didn't have time.

Mrs Lavender picked him up, resting him against her purple cardigan, which smelled of flowers. It smelled, in fact, like Bluebell Wood, and cruelly reminded Barney of being nine years old and with his parents on a long Sunday walk.

'Right, class, please settle down. I'd better just tell Miss Whipmire about this.'

And she carried Barney out of the room, stroking the back of his head tenderly, without the faintest clue that she was, in fact, taking him to the office of a murderer.

The Unknowable Miss Whipmire

As we have already discussed, Miss Whipmire was the scariest head teacher in the whole of Blandfordshire. You only had to say her name out loud to change the temperature to a few degrees below freezing. But, actually, the strangest thing was how little people knew about her.

True, they knew what she looked like.

They knew she was a very skinny, very tall woman. Basically a skin-wrapped skeleton with glasses that sat at the end of her nose so she could always look down at whoever was speaking to her.

They also knew she looked quite old. In fact, she looked about two hundred. But obviously she wasn't. She was just living on Misery Time. (If you don't already know, Misery Time means that miserable people get old very much quicker than happy people. Sour thoughts inside your head apparently make it look like a pickled walnut quite quickly.)

Of course, she did smile from time to time. At

parents. And school governors. But she didn't *like* smiling. It actually seemed to hurt her, but it was just something she had to do now and then to stay in her job.

People knew she drove to school in the slick silver car she had bought several months ago, but no one had been to her house since around the time she had been promoted to head teacher. No one had been invited, and they would have probably made an excuse even if they had.

Apparently, before Barney had arrived at the school, Miss Whipmire had been quite a nice and caring teacher. Back when she was just a deputy head. Someone who only raised her voice when absolutely necessary and never stared at anyone as if they were a dirty mark that needed rubbing out, which was how she now looked at the children in her school.

But a few days after she became head teacher, she changed. And everybody could see she looked crosser.

No one knew where that anger had come from. They just assumed it had something to do with her becoming the head.

But then, as I said, no one knew very much about Miss Whipmire. And certainly not Mrs Lavender, who had now arrived with the cat at Miss Whipmire's office door.

She knocked. Waited nervously. Like everyone else, she was scared of her boss. Indeed, only last night she had woken up in a cold sweat from a nightmare in which Miss Whipmire had called her to her office for placing too many ticks on pupils' homework.

'You want ticks, I'll give you *ticks*,' she'd said in the dream, unleashing a whole army of fleas and leaving poor Mrs Lavender on the floor, itching like mad.

And she wasn't the only one who was nervous now. Barney too was deeply scared. Admittedly, he'd never felt happy standing outside Miss Whipmire's office, but this time he felt even worse than usual. His fur was standing on end and his whiskers were twitching with nervous anticipation.

He was sensing something. But he didn't know exactly what it was he sensed.

You see, when you first become a cat you have a lot of cat senses, but the trouble is, you don't know how to use them or understand what they mean. It's like hearing a foreign language. You hear the words but can't translate them. All Barney knew was that his claws were out and he was clinging to Mrs Lavender for dear life.

The door handle turned.

A moment later there she was, staring at the cat,

intrigued. Maybe even a little hopeful.

'What is this?'

'It's a cat,' said Mrs Lavender. 'I'm ever so sorry for disturbing you. It's just I don't know what to do with it. It came into my classroom.'

'Your *classroom*? Well, I've always told you, Mrs Lavender, that you have a habit of making children act like animals, but this really is a step further, isn't it?'

Mrs Lavender didn't know if Miss Whipmire was joking. So she gave a very quiet laugh, hidden at the back of her throat like a dead mouse under a rug.

'I thought it best to bring it to you,' she said, 'so you could maybe, possibly, perhaps call someone like animal welfare or a cat-rescue centre, or something.'

Miss Whipmire sucked in air through her nostrils, the way she always did when she was about to get furious. But she didn't. She was too clever. 'Absolutely. You are quite right, Mrs Lavender. You couldn't be any more right if I sawed you in half and stole the whole left side of your body. I will indeed call the necessary authorities.'

'Right.'

And then there was a very long silence. Long enough for Barney to say his prayers and for Miss Whipmire to bark at a late Year Eight shuffling to class and having

a nose at what was going on. 'If you want your eyes
to take a holiday from their sockets, keep staring, you
dopey slug,' she said as the boy turned away in fear.

'That was a little bit unfair, wasn't it?' said Mrs
Lavender in the poor boy's defence.

'I certainly hope so.'

'But—'

'Mrs Lavender, these children – all human children

– are despicable brutes. They are poisonous weeds. If you water them with kindness, well, there goes the nice garden. Trim them, snip them, cut them down, that's the best way.'

After which, Barney was grabbed roughly by the scruff of his furry neck and yanked from Mrs Lavender's cardigan and its smell of warm summer meadows into Miss Whipmire's thin, unloving arms.

As Barney was stroked too hard he imagined Miss Whipmire giving one of her painful smiles as she said, 'Don't worry, I'll see to it. You can go now.'

And he watched Mrs Lavender turn and walk away, the sound of her footsteps echoing and fading along the corridor until they were gone completely.

A Strange Discovery

Barney was standing on a chair, where Miss Whipmire had placed him. It was the same chair he'd sat in yesterday when he'd imagined life couldn't get any worse. How wrong he'd been. He watched as his skeletal head teacher went over and locked the door, wondering why she needed to do that.

She turned and gave him a strange look. Not friendly, obviously, but not cross, either.

'Who are you?' she whispered.

Of course, people ask animals things all the time. Like if a dog decides to go to the toilet on a carpet you might ask, 'What is the matter with you?' Or if a goldfish is lying upside down on the top of the water its owner might enquire, 'Are you dead?' But when a human asks a member of another species a question, they don't normally expect an answer, just as Rissa hadn't this morning.

But Barney really thought an answer was exactly what Miss Whipmire expected.

She walked over, leaned right into Barney's face. 'Don't just sit there. *Tell me*. I need to be sure.'

She's mad, Barney thought as he smelled her fishy breath.

'Well,' he said, assuming she wouldn't understand. 'I'm not a cat really. I'm Barney Willow. And, by the way, you are the most horrible head teacher in the universe.'

He expected her to look blank.

He was talking cat, not human.

But she wasn't blank. She was smiling – without any sign of pain. And soon the smile was a laugh, and the laugh grew until the sound of it filled the room. It was a horrible laugh. The kind of laugh reserved for witches to use over cauldrons after casting an evil spell. But Miss Whipmire wasn't a witch. Not a real one, anyway. She was something else, something just as strange. And twice as evil.

She was now putting her hand over her mouth and trying desperately to keep the laugh locked inside, but she couldn't. She was soon on the floor, curled right up, laughing uncontrollably.

'He did it!' she was saying to Barney's confusion. 'He actually did it.'

About a minute later she stood up. 'Oh, that's

funny. That's so *satisfying* . . . Barney Willow! You're
Barney Willow!'

Barney waited, wondering whether to speak again,
but before he knew it, words were leaking from him:
'Yes, I am. How can you understand me?'

Miss Whipmire had understood his miaow – hence
the speech marks (and, yes, all those words equalled
only one miaow) – but she chose not to answer it. Not
right then, anyway.

'When?' she said, on the brink of more laughter. 'What?'

'Still as slow as ever, aren't you, Barney Willow? I'll ask it slowly.' She closed her eyes and moved her mouth carefully around her words. 'When. Did. You. Become. A. Cat?'

'This morning,' he said. 'I felt funny for a while, but it was only this morning that I became . . . like this.'

(Three miaows, long and heartfelt.)

'This morning . . . this morning . . .' said Miss Whipmire, thinking, and tapping her fingers on her chin as if it were a silent piano.

And then she had another question. 'And so, where are you?'

Barney was confused. 'I'm here.'

'No, you imbecile, the *other* you. The *better* you. The cat in your body.'

'I don't know. He was walking to the bus stop with Rissa and then he ran away.'

'Good.' Miss Whipmire nodded the kind of nod you give when everything is going to plan. 'Good, good. He'll be taking some time to adjust, like I told him to. Then he'll be on his way here. Very good . . . But not for you, obviously. Bad, *bad* for you. Because there goes your ticket.'

'What ticket?' said Barney, noticing an envelope on the desk with what looked like tickets sticking out.

'Oh, not these,' she said, waving the envelope. He could see the address:

Miss Polly Whipmire
63 Sycamore Terrace
Blandford
Blandfordshire
BL1 3NR

'These are real tickets – my tickets. Mine and my only love's. Out of here for ever. This time tomorrow I'll be en route to Old Siam – Thailand. I'm talking about the ticket back to you. Back to *you* you.'

'I don't understand.'

'Of course you don't,' she said, her thin lips curling into a frosty smile. 'After all, just because you look like a cat doesn't mean you have the brain of a cat, does it?' She leaned close into him again. He felt his claws growing, itching to strike her nose. But he was too scared to do anything.

'Do you know what the IQ of the average cat is?' she asked him.

'No.'

'One thousand and six. That's nine hundred and six points higher than the average human.' Miss Whipmire paused, licked her lips as if savouring the taste of something. 'Anyway, this happens more than you think. See, I'm a cat. *Was* a cat. Oh yes, that's right – Blandford High School has had a Siamese cat acting as its head teacher for quite a while now.' She smiled again as Barney began to absorb the madness of what she was telling him. 'And do you know what? This school has never had such good results!'

Sardines

Barney felt his new thick black hair rise all over his body.

Miss Whipmire was a *cat*!

'Oh yes, true as a tail, as we cats say,' she said, popping behind the desk and opening up a drawer. She pulled out a tin of sardines.

'Do you know how many sardines you can buy on a headteacher's salary?' she asked, peeling off the lid and placing one of the oily fish into her mouth.

'No, I don't,' Barney told her, remembering the smell of fish he'd noticed yesterday as a human sitting right here in her office. The smell that was stronger still now that he had cat nostrils.

'A lot,' she said, making no attempt to close her mouth as she chewed the fish. '*Mmmmmmm*, delicious. Better than cat food, I can tell you. *Eugh*. Cat food. That's what I *used* to live on. And not just any cat food. The most disgusting cat food in the whole of Costslicers Supermarket – rabbit kidney.'

Miss Whipmire looked like she was about to be sick at the memory. But she became angry instead and beat her human fist down on her desk causing the pens in her weird pen pot to bounce about.

'You see, everyone thought that Miss Whip-mire – the *real* Miss Whipmire – was so *lovely*,' she said bitterly. 'Lovely Polly Whipmire! Even after two days in the job it was clear she was going to be a terrible head teacher, but no one minded, because she was such a *wonderful* person. Riding her little bicycle, being *gentle* and *kind* with all the children, loving her little Siamese cat . . .' She shook her head. 'Well, that's not how I saw it. Not with her rabbit liver, and the tiny kitchen she used to shut me in.'

She ate another sardine, and another, and one more, the last while she closed her eyes, comforting herself with the taste.

119

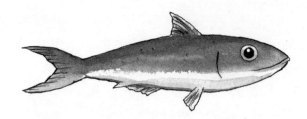

'But she doesn't bother me now,' she said in a most peculiar voice. A voice which sounded as cold as a grave in the night. 'Oh, no, you don't bother me now, do you, Polly?'

Barney realized she was no longer looking at him. She was gazing down at the table. At first he thought she was staring at the empty tin of sardines she had just placed there.

But no.

She was staring at the pen pot next to it. The funny-shaped black one with the holes. She leaned forward, took one of the school pens; the ones that said: BLANDFORD HIGH SCHOOL – YOUR CHILD IS OUR WORLD. And then she studied Barney's face as she tapped the pen against the pot. The pot shaped like a skull.

A cat's skull, he thought as he began to realize exactly what Miss Whipmire – or rather this cat who had *become* Miss Whipmire – was truly capable of.

Poor Polly

'Of course, I had to cut the top of the skull off,' Miss Whipmire explained thoughtfully, admiring her handiwork. 'And I painted it, to disguise it. But it works quite well. What do you think?'

'I . . . I . . . I . . . think you're a monster.'

She shook her head. 'No, Barney, I can assure you the former Miss Whipmire had a very nice time in my ageing cat body. I told her lovely stories of Old Siam, and I kept her warm and safe.' She sighed thoughtfully. 'Of course, I didn't give her anything to eat or drink, but then, compared to the rabbit kidney she used to give me, I was doing her a favour really. Oh, poor Polly, though. Fading away like that. It was hard. I do still have this lovely little memento to keep me company.'

She tapped the pot again.

Her mouth twitched at the corners, like a cat's tail. 'The trouble is, I do have rather a lot of pens. I get them free. One of the perks of the job. But this old head isn't very big.' Her mouth twitched its way into a smile again. 'I suppose what I'm really saying is that I could do with a new pen pot. Do you understand?'

And, just in case Barney *didn't* understand, she tapped the side of her head, then pointed at him. 'And I think yours would hold a few more. Yes, I might even get some marker pens in there.'

'You're mad,' Barney said as he leaped down and began to walk backwards towards the door. 'You're absolutely mad.'

'No, I'll tell you what would have been mad,' she hissed. 'Staying a cat. Now *that* would have been crazy. To be a cat, that's no fun . . . What I went through at the hands of humans . . . When I was just little old Caramel, well . . . And not just with Polly Whipmire, either. Oh no, she was the least of it. You see, Polly had neighbours, and the neighbours had children. The Freemans. Torturers, they were. Once, on bonfire night, they . . . they—'

She stopped. Closed her eyes tight shut, as though the memory was a piece of sharp glass in her shoe.

'Well, put it this way. I left the house that night with a tail and came back without one. And, of course, I was relieved when I heard the Freemans were moving abroad, to Thailand – my ancestral homeland, as it happens. But my sadness remained, every time I turned round and saw the space where my tail should have been.

'Anyway, I could have coped with all that . . . I could have coped with anything if I had been with . . .'

She stopped for a second, took a deep breath, and carried on. 'As I was saying, the day I lost my tail I vowed to get my revenge on them, the humans, *all* humans, especially children. So I remembered one of those stories I was telling you about, passed down from my ancestors in Old Siam. The story of the cat who became a king. A king who terrorized the humans who had cooked his parents. Well, not many children are scared of kings these days . . . but a head teacher? That was perfect, especially as I *lived* with someone who had just become one!'

Barney's tail rubbed up against the door. He had to get out of the room before Miss Whipmire finished her story (we shall keep calling her Miss Whipmire, by the way, because calling her by her cat name, Caramel, makes you think of a nice, soothing, sweet and sugary sort of taste, which isn't really appropriate). But how could Barney escape? The door was locked. The window was closed, and too high to reach, anyway. It was hopeless.

Please don't hurt me.

Miss Whipmire didn't listen to him. She just stood up and walked out from behind her desk as upright and perfectly postured as a ballet dancer, taking careful steps in Barney's direction.

'So I waited until she had a bad day in her new demanding job. I didn't have to wait long. And I knew what to do. I knew I had to make my life look very, very easy. So I stretched out on the rug by the fire, and eventually it came. The wish. And I thought of what the humans had taken from me and I wished right back, thinking of how I could make everything right again.'

Barney could hear pupils out on the playing fields getting ready for the first rugby match of the day. For once he wished he could be out there among them. 'But I was never cruel to any cat,' Barney miaowed.

'You are a human, no matter what you look like,' Miss Whipmire said in a voice as cold as morning frost. 'And to a human a cat is just a cat, and an ant is just an ant, and a tree is just a tree. So I'm just like you: I judge the cake on a single slice. You are a human boy, and so you deserve punishment, like all the other human boys.'

'But why me in particular? You've always picked on me – why?'

'Oh, you want a *motive*, how *sweet*. How very human. Well, I can give you one if that will make you happy. I remember things. I remember being a young cat and chased by a King Charles spaniel in the park. I remember a vile little freckle-faced boy laughing and not even bothering to call for his dog. There. What about that?'

Barney pictured the scene. 'But I wasn't laughing at the cat . . . I mean, you . . . I was laughing at Guster, my dog. And I was laughing because I knew he couldn't catch you. He's only a little spaniel. He's never caught a cat in his life. He wasn't going to hurt . . .'

But even as he was saying this, in feeble, weak miaows, he was thinking of Guster's giant face looking down at him this morning, a face that had been ready to kill. He hadn't looked like such a 'little spaniel' then.

'I'm sorry,' Barney pleaded.

'Oh, you will be. Later, when I take you home and get working on my new pen pot . . .'

Barney could hear footsteps walk by in the corridor outside the door. The familiar *clip-clop* of the high heels worn by the school secretary, whose name Barney didn't know.

Help! he called. *Help! Help!*

He was desperate. But maybe there were other

former cats working at the school, ones that weren't evil. And, anyway, even if there weren't, maybe people would worry about a miaowing cat behind a shut door. Miss Whipmire certainly seemed to think so.

'Sssh!' she said in one of her shout whispers, crouching with her arms out wide in case Barney tried to run. 'Silence!'

Help! Help!

Her hands reached towards him, her nails as long as claws.

Outside, the footsteps stopped. Not faded. Stopped.

This concerned Miss Whipmire.

And then it came. A gentle knock on the door, no louder than a rat's head-butt.

Miss Whipmire sighed, furious. 'Yes?' Then she placed a finger to her lips, telling Barney to be silent. But Barney knew this might be his last chance.

Help! he miaowed as loud as he possibly could, and it came out as a kind of distressed *aghow* sound which would be hard for a cat-loving human to ignore.

'It's just . . . I heard what sounded like a cat,' said the secretary from beyond the closed door.

Miss Whipmire rolled her eyes. Then gave in. She opened the door.

'No, Daphne, you didn't hear a cat,' she snapped.

'Now, please disappear and do some secretary-ing. Go. Type something.'

Barney didn't wait another second. The door wasn't going to be open long, after all. So he ran, or started to run.

But Miss Whipmire must have seen him and, with some of her Siamese cat reflexes still intact, quickly opened the door wider, squashing Barney's middle against a filing cabinet.

'I . . . can't . . . breathe,' Barney gasped.

'What was that noise?' asked Daphne, trying to peer inside Miss Whipmire's office.

'It's the heating system,' Miss Whipmire lied. 'It's playing up. Something's gone wrong with the pipes. I've called a man about it. Now, if that's all . . .'

'Yes,' said Daphne. 'I'm sorry for disturbing you.'

Barney felt hope disappear. The air arrived back in his lungs with the close of the door. While he was still coughing he felt Miss Whipmire's long nails dig into the back of his neck and lift him high into the air.

'Now, have a little look out of the window,' she told Barney with fake tenderness. 'It will be the last time you'll see daylight, I should imagine.'

Barney caught a glimpse of boys playing rugby, and the trees beyond lining the road. Cars swooshing by. Still, white clouds teasing him like a happy dream. A second later it was all gone. He was dropped, landing on a cold metal surface next to an old paper file. He looked up and saw Miss Whipmire's face staring down at him, smiling as if she were doing him a favour. 'We all end up in the dark sooner or later,' she said. Then she pushed the drawer of the filing cabinet shut, leaving Barney in the darkest blackness he'd ever known.

Inside the Filing Cabinet

So, this was a great start to being twelve. Turning into a cat and getting locked inside his psychotic, post-feline head teacher's filing cabinet.

'Let me out!'

Then her voice, as cold and hard as the metal that contained him. 'Oh, I'm sorry, but really you should thank me. You see, I'm doing what I'm paid to do. I'm educating you. I'm giving a lesson in horror, and teaching you that you should really be careful what you wish for. Oh, and that thing about cats having nine lives, well, that's a lie. As you'll find out when I take you home with me.'

'But my mum! It's not fair on her. My dad's already missing. If I go missing too she'll have nobody.'

'You're forgetting one thing,' said Miss Whipmire. 'You're a cat. So even if I set you free – which, by the way, won't happen – your mum won't ever know it's you, will she? And you won't ever be able to change back because you are too weak.'

'Wait . . . I can change back?' Barney asked.

'No, imbecile. Did you not hear me?'

'Yes, I did, but you said I couldn't change back because I was weak. Which means if I was strong enough, I could—'

'It doesn't matter if you live to a hundred (which you won't, being a cat) – you will NEVER be strong enough.'

Barney had no idea what she was talking about, although he was beginning to sense Miss Whipmire's motives weren't solely to do with revenge. 'But you're saying there *is* a way to turn back?'

He could feel her smile, even though he couldn't see it. 'Unfortunately for you, that's very unlikely. You see, the cat who turned into you is going to be happier being you than you ever were. You've swapped bodies with a cat who hates humans just as much as me, Barney Willow. There is no return ticket for you.'

Barney wondered if she was lying. Or if there really was no way back to being human.

'You see,' continued Miss Whipmire, 'you've missed your opportunity. Because that is what life is. A grand opportunity. And opportunities are like cat flaps. They don't stay open for ever . . . But don't worry too much about it. The dead don't have regrets.'

Miss Whipmire seemed amused by these words.

Barney had no choice but to stay there, standing on paperclips, with nothing except the darkness and the smell of stationery and the petrifying sound of a cat's laugh coming from a human mouth.

After that there was silence.

Barney waited and waited, trying to think of a plan.

None came.

Even when he heard Miss Whipmire leave the room for a while, Barney didn't know what he could do. There was no way he could push open a locked drawer from the inside, and with paws instead of fingers he wouldn't have much hope trying to pick a lock with paperclips.

So he miaowed, continuously, until he was exhausted, until the darkness made his eyes so heavy he could hardly keep them open. But he kept on miaowing, in a state which was somewhere between napping and awake as he heard, very faintly, his long-lost father's voice rising from a dream.

It will be all right, it will be all right, it will be all right . . .

The Heroic Return of the Author

Hello. Only me. The author again. I've been trying to keep out of the way, letting the story get on by itself (you've got to let the little darlings go eventually), and it's been doing all right, I think. Only a couple of little slips, but it's back on its feet. Anyway, I just thought now was the right time to point out number seven. Remember? From the first chapter? That list I gave you. Well, I thought now would be the time to spell it out.

CROSS-SPECIES TWO-WAY METAMORPHOSIS.

That is to say, the ability a cat has to turn into a human, and to turn that human into the cat they once were. So, for example, Caramel became Miss Whipmire and the original Miss Whipmire became Caramel – and then, erm, a pen pot.

Oh, but wait, you're thinking. (No, you are, honestly.) *If cats could turn into humans they'd say so.*

Well, here's a question. If someone came up to you and said they used to be a cat, would you believe them?

Would you say, 'Oh, that's nice. You used to be a cat, I used to hate mushrooms, wow, let's be friends'?

I doubt it.

You would say, 'No, you didn't used to be a cat because that's *impossible*. You are obviously a little bit mad and I think I'd better go home now. Bye-bye.'

You might not actually say it out loud. You look too nice and polite for that. But that's what you'd be thinking.

So, cats who are now humans and *have* mentioned it haven't been believed. And those who don't mention it haven't been asked. And as for those humans who have turned into cats, well, they often tell people about it but no one's listening. It's just one lonely miaow after another.

OK, that's me done. I'm out of here. I'm dropping the story back off at school and letting it fend for itself. Go on, story, off you go.

Be good.

History

Rissa Fairweather liked history.

It wasn't her favourite subject. Her favourite subject was science. Well, not all science. Just the stuff about what makes stars glimmer and the stuff which tells you that every time you look up at the night sky you are looking at the past, at stars that have actually existed since before the dinosaurs, before history itself.

But history was interesting too. As interesting as art and music, her other favourites. And the Vikings, whom Mr Crust was talking about today, were particularly good fun – with their long-boats and axes and outdoor toilets and bloody violence.

But today she wasn't paying any attention. Instead she just kept thinking about the empty chair next to her and the same recurring questions. Why *had* Barney run off like that? And why hadn't he said a word when she'd walked up the street with him?

Maybe he was sad about his dad. She remembered when Barney had found out his dad had gone missing.

He had been quiet for weeks then. Far quieter than when his parents had got divorced, because there were so many uncertainties. Had his dad run away? Been kidnapped? Died in a ditch where no one could find him?

These were questions which could probably grow and grow inside a boy's head until they stopped words altogether. And Barney, in those last few months at primary school, had been very quiet indeed.

Rissa wasn't at all convinced that Barney was over it, even now.

'Rissa, am I boring you?'

For a moment Rissa stopped thinking about Barney's possible troubles and looked up to see Mr Crust's wrinkled face staring straight at her.

'No, sir,' she said.

'Good, well, perhaps you'd like to tell us about runestones, then?'

'I'm sorry. My mind was wandering—'

The class giggled but Rissa didn't care.

Rissa's mum always said: 'No one can make you feel bad about yourself without your consent.' Which meant that you can't control what people said about you, but you can control how you *feel* about what they said. Oh, and if Rissa was ever really stressed, she followed her dad's advice and spoke the magic calming word under her breath.

Marmalade.

And Rissa had repeated all this to Barney, many times, but she knew he wasn't like her. She could always feel his shame whenever Gavin called him 'Weeping Willow', after the time he found Barney wiping away a tear on his missing dad's birthday.

But Rissa knew she had a lot to be thankful for, and that helped. She knew that however tough the day turned out to be, she would go home to her parents and they would cheer her up by singing songs (her dad was very good at playing the acoustic guitar) and, on clear nights, talk about the constellations that were seen through her telescope. Or, failing that, they would eat home-made chilli bean burgers and hand-cut chips, followed by one of her mum's delicious carrot cakes made with a dollop of her special ingredient – marmalade.

That was all you needed to be happy.

Food. Music. A clear night sky and a telescope.

Plus love.

Lots and lots of love.

Meanwhile Mr Crust was still talking:

'. . . Runestones are usually stones that were put

into the ground by Vikings to remember important battles or men who had died. They have mainly been found in Scandinavia, but there have been some located in the British Isles, such as Northumbria and the Isle of Man. And a picture of the battles or dead men would be engraved onto the stone. But sometimes these "runic inscriptions", as they are called, would be a picture of an animal. Horses were commonly depicted as they often died in battles with their owners. But there were other animals too. There are, for instance, a surprising number of runestones dedicated to cats. And you might think this is sweet, but the strange thing is that, although cats were sometimes kept by Vikings to kill rodents, they weren't really pets. So it remains a complete mystery to historians and archaeologists . . .'

Mr Crust's ramblings reminded Rissa of the cat that had come to school with her this morning. And, for some strange reason she couldn't identify, this made her think of Barney again.

Something was definitely wrong. Barney had never run off like that before. Why would he have done that? What had scared him so much?

The questions stayed there, hovering, until the bell rang.

Lunch hour.

In the dining hall Rissa sat at a table on her own, eating the only vegetarian option – cheese and tomato pizza made with what was meant to be white bread, but tasted more like bath sponge. Well, she was on her own until Petra and Petula Primm came over to sit with her.

The twins were very neat-looking girls with shiny black hair cut into two perfectly immaculate bobs. And they were absolutely identical, except that Petra always wore a school tie while Petula, like most other girls, went for an open collar. They never normally

139

made any effort with Rissa, as Petra and Petula didn't like the idea of someone who lived on a barge, especially as they lived in a very large house near the library, full of everything they ever asked their daddy for. Today, though, they seemed very interested in talking to her.

'What happened to Barney this morning?' asked Petra instantly, placing her tray on the table.

'Why did he run away?' added Petula, doing the same.

Rissa shrugged and swallowed some more bath sponge. 'I don't know. It's weird.' She thought about whether she should really say the next thing. But she did. 'I think it might have something to do with his dad.'

She noticed the twins look at each other, their eyes shining with secret knowledge.

'What made you—' started Petula.

'Say that?' finished Petra.

'Well, I don't know. I just think he might be missing his dad.'

'Or,' suggested Petra, allowing Petula to continue, 'He might have *seen* his dad.'

Rissa swallowed her food and stared at the twins. She knew they were itching to tell her something. 'His dad's *missing*,' she said. 'No one's seen him for months.'

The twins gave each other that look again.

'Let's show her,' said Petra.

'Yes.' Petula was positively bursting with excitement. '*Let's.*'

And the twins both got out their identical mobile phones as menacingly as if they were weapons. They were incredibly shiny and sparkly and had their initials, 'PP', engraved on the back.

Rissa watched, worried, as the twins' thumbs kept sliding across their screens.

'There!' said Petula.

'Me too!' said Petra.

And they both turned their phones round for Rissa to view the photo on each screen. The photo on Petula's phone was of a man with a beard, but it was a bit blurry and dark so Rissa couldn't really tell what she was supposed to be seeing.

The photo on Petra's phone was much clearer. It was of the same man. A man with mid-brown hair and the same big bushy beard. He was sitting at some kind of counter, and there was a painting on the wall behind. It was an oil painting of a cat.

But it wasn't the painting she was meant to be looking at.

It was the man.

She knew him from somewhere, but couldn't think where.

'Take away the beard and who do you have?' asked Petra.

Rissa gasped as she imagined the man without a beard. She remembered the face from primary school. Could picture the man at sports day cheering on Barney as he struggled in the sack race. *No. It couldn't be.*

But then Petula took something from her pocket – a piece of folded paper – and slid it across the table towards Rissa. Rissa unfolded it and saw it was an old newspaper cutting from the *Blandford Gazette*.

'It was in our dad's paper,' said Petula, reminding Rissa that their father was the *Blandford Gazette*'s editor in chief.

'What is it?' she asked.

But Rissa didn't need an answer. She'd unfolded it now and could see it was a photo of a man she recognized, this time in black and white. And underneath the photo was the man's name, and a brief summary of the news story.

Neil Willow, aged 45, went missing two days ago from his home on Bradbury Drive. He lived alone, having separated from his wife several months earlier. No one has any idea where he went.

'Barney's dad,' said Rissa.

'And read that,' Petula told her.

But Petra was already doing so with delicious glee. '*No one has any idea where he went!*' she said. Then added: 'Until *now!*'

And that's when Rissa looked again at the photos on the twins' mobile phones, then back to the newspaper cutting.

'Take away the beard and who is it?' asked Petula. 'And we only took these pictures yesterday . . . so you know what that means, don't you?'

There was no denying it. It was the same man. The same eyes, the same nose, the same everything.

'So, Barney's dad is still alive . . . ?' said Rissa in shock.

The twins nodded, thrilled.

'We stayed with our aunt at the weekend, and we were at the cattery near her house. She was picking up her cat. It's in Edgarton, fifteen miles away. That is where Mr Willow is working.'

'It's going to be the best story ever. Too good for the school newspaper,' added Petula. 'Daddy's promised us that if we uncover the mystery we can be his star journalists. We'll have our own front-page story in the *Blandford Gazette*!'

But Rissa was hardly listening. She was just thinking about Barney's weird behaviour that morning, and how there must be a link to this.

Of course, what the Primms were telling her should have been good news. But as they kept on smiling, Rissa's stomach tightened with dread.

Something was wrong with all this, she just knew it.

And so she put down her knife and fork, said goodbye to the twins, and left the hall with urgent steps.

Rissa's Decision

Rissa didn't particularly like Miss Whipmire.

Of course she didn't. *No one* liked Miss Whipmire. She was, quite simply, impossible to like, in the same way bath-sponge pizza was impossible to enjoy.

But Miss Whipmire was the head teacher, and the job of a head teacher is to *know what to do . . .*

That is what Mrs Lavender told Rissa when she went to tell her about Barney. At first, and on Rissa's insistence, Mrs Lavender had tried to phone Barney's mum at the library, but it was engaged.

'Now, if you are still worried you must, absolutely *must*, go and tell Miss Whipmire.'

Rissa had made a face at this. 'But she doesn't like Barney.'

'Oh, don't be silly. Of course she does. And even if she doesn't, I'm sure she wouldn't want anything bad to happen to him . . . You know our school motto: "Your child is our world". Miss Whipmire came up with that herself.'

So Rissa reluctantly agreed and walked the empty corridors towards the head teacher's office, knowing she would be there – one of the odd things about Miss Whipmire was that she never seemed to *eat*, and she certainly didn't join the other teachers in the dining hall with their school dinners and packed lunches. But then, Rissa didn't know about her sardine drawer.

She arrived. Outside the door.

She waited nervously, and whispered under her breath.

'Marmalade, marmalade, marmalade.'

Then she knocked.

There came an angry squawk from beyond the door. 'Ye-es?'

'Hello . . . it's Rissa Fairweather. I'm . . . I'm a pupil here. Year Seven. I just . . . want to speak to you about something. Mrs Lavender said to . . . to see you.'

'Not *now*!'

Rissa started to walk away from the door. But she stopped. Barney might be in trouble, and she had to do everything she could. So she went back, looked around to make sure no one was listening, then said in as confident a voice as she could manage: 'It's about Barney Willow.'

And the door opened so fast Rissa jumped.

'Come inside,' hissed Miss Whipmire, with angry fear bulging her eyes. '*Now!*'

The Howling Miaow

Rissa stepped inside Miss Whipmire's office as the door was closed – and then *locked* – behind her. She had never been in here before and she found it a strange place. The scent of fish, the cat calendar, the unusual plants, the poster of a dark-looking, exotic landscape on the back of the door (*Chao Phraya – Thailand* it said on it), the sheepskin rug that was draped over Miss Whipmire's chair, the ugly pot with the pens nearly falling out of it. Somehow the office didn't feel part of the school, the way a wart on a finger doesn't feel like a true part of a hand.

'What *about* Barney Willow?' Miss Whipmire said, turning to give Rissa a vicious stare.

'He's . . . erm, he's not at school today.'

'Oh, so you're telling tales. It's true what they say – no loyalty among rats or children.'

'No. I'm just worried about him.'

'Why? He's a despicable boy. One of the worst.

And boys are a despicable breed so that is really saying something.'

'No,' said Rissa, feeling her voice waiver. 'He's not. He's a good friend. The best, in fact. I just wondered whether there was anything we . . . or *you* could do?'

Miss Whipmire hesitated. She was looking worriedly at the filing cabinet for some reason Rissa couldn't understand. Then she softened her tone. 'Lots of boys aren't at school today – and girls. Without meaning any offence, you are all lazy slugs. I wouldn't worry your mollusky head about it.'

Rissa heard something. Or thought she did. A faint but sad kind of a howl. It was a noise that made Miss Whipmire's face stiffen. But then it faded, so Rissa decided to finish what she had come to say. 'I saw Barney this morning. But he was weird. Quiet. Didn't say a word. And then, just as we were heading to the bus stop, he ran away.'

'Oh, that is strange,' Miss Whipmire said, smiling one of her agonizing smiles. 'Well, don't worry, I assure you I will do absolutely everything to look into this. Now, if you'd please excuse me . . . I'd better start making some phone calls.'

Rissa felt reluctant to leave the room. There was something peculiar and rather fake about Miss

Whipmire's sudden switch to concern. Rissa suspected that she didn't care about anything except getting her out of the office.

Indeed, Miss Whipmire had the door wide open, gesturing for Rissa to leave. But she waited. 'I've tried to phone Barney's mum but I haven't been able to speak to her yet.'

Again, she thought very hard about whether she should say the next thing. But she did, because she knew it would be even more difficult to say it to Mrs Willow, and because she wanted Miss Whipmire to understand the seriousness of the situation.

'Just one more thing,' she began. 'It's Barney's father. He's alive and people know where he is. He's working at a cattery in Edgarton. I've just seen a photo of him. I'm worried that this has got something to do with Barney's weird behaviour.'

Miss Whipmire didn't look at all surprised by this information. But her eyebrows pulled together rather crossly, as though she was annoyed with such knowledge being spoken aloud in front of the filing cabinet. 'Right, well, I'm sure that's a load of nonsense . . .' she said, and tried to shoo Rissa out of the room with a string of 'all right's and 'I'll see what I can do's.

But then it came.

That noise again.

Only this time it was unmistakable.

A howling miaow. A *cat's* miaow. And it was coming from the filing cabinet.

The Voices in the Dark

In the dark of the filing cabinet Barney had heard every word.

His dad!

Alive!

The thoughts definitely came with exclamation marks, but they soon became questions.

His dad?

Alive?

And the biggest of all was: if his dad *was* still alive, why had he never visited or called or emailed to say he was OK?

But whatever the answer, it wasn't going to be found on the inside of a filing cabinet. Nor would it be found if Barney was dead.

So he miaowed the loudest miaow he could manage, one which hurt his new, dry cat throat and took all the breath from his reduced lungs. But one which did the job.

He heard them now.

First Rissa. Nervous. 'What was that?'

Then Miss Whipmire. Maybe just a little nervous too at first: 'What was what?'

'That noise. It sounded like a—'

'Faulty heating system?'

'No. Actually, it sounded like a . . . like a cat.'

Barney miaowed again. *Help! Rissa, it's me! I'm here!*

'That was definitely a *cat*!' Rissa said.

'You misheard. Now go back to class.'

'It's lunch hour. I don't have a class.'

'Well, if you don't leave this office I will have to write to your parents.'

Ha! thought Barney. Miss Whipmire obviously didn't know Rissa – or her parents, for that matter – if she thought the threat of a letter home was going to stop her.

'With all due respect,' said Rissa, 'my mum and dad would be more upset with me if I left a cat in a filing cabinet than if you sent a letter home . . .' Barney then heard her mutter something under her breath. 'Marmalade, marmalade, marmalade.'

Go, Rissa! Barney miaowed, proud of his best friend.

'Would you keep your voice down!' hushed Miss Whipmire, shutting the door again. Or trying to. But she obviously caught the eye of Mr Waffler, who must have been walking past.

'Is everything all right, Miss Whipmire?' Barney heard him ask in his deep voice.

'Yes,' she said, as fast and sharp as a pair of scissors. 'And it has absolutely nothing to do with you, Mr Waffler! Nothing! Whatsoever! Go back to your Shakespeare.'

Mr Waffler shuffled off. The door closed fully. But Rissa had the upper hand now.

'There's a cat in the filing cabinet,' she said, and Barney could feel his friend's determination pushing her on. 'And I have a feeling it is the cat Mrs Lavender gave to you. The one that followed me to school. And I don't know why it would be . . . where it is . . . and I know you are my head teacher and I should do as you say, but I believe in animal rights and I believe cats and human beings have an equal right not to be locked away in the dark.'

Miss Whipmire snapped. 'They are *not* equal! Cats are far superior to idiotic humans like you!'

'Well,' said Rissa, 'if you actually believed that you would not be keeping one in a cupboard!'

And then Barney heard Miss Whipmire nearly come out with truth. 'That is *not* a—'

Go on, say it!

Tell her!

Tell her! Tell her! Tell her I'm not a cat!

'Not a what?' asked Rissa.

Miss Whipmire quickly covered her mistake. 'Not a cupboard. It's a cabinet. It's a human distinction, but I am a human so—'

Rissa pulled a puzzled face. 'Well, whatever it's called, would you open it for me so I can have a look?'

There was silence, but Barney could feel the tension in his whiskers. Then the voices came back, but muffled, even for Barney's cat ears.

It went quiet again.

Barney waited. Didn't even miaow. Whatever was going to happen was going to happen. He would stay in the dark and wait for whatever Miss Whipmire planned to do to him. Or he would come out into safety, to Rissa.

155

After what felt like a hundred beats of his fast and tiny heart he heard Miss Whipmire's voice. 'You will regret this, girl, I promise you.'

And then Barney heard the lock turn, and, as the drawer opened with a metallic whisper, he was back out in the light and in the arms of his best friend, who whispered warmly, 'marmalade' into his ear.

'Breathe so much as a word about this little misunderstanding and I will make your life hell,' said Miss Whipmire. 'Trust me, no one will believe the words of a scruffy twelve-year-old girl over her head teacher.'

As he was carried out of the door, Barney stared back over Rissa's arm. He could just about see Miss Whipmire staring at him, pointing to the skull pen pot and mouthing the words, 'You're next!'

A Bad Feeling

Rissa walked out of school, out of the gates, and Barney noticed (though Rissa didn't) that Pumpkin was still there on the pavement. And the ginger cat was still staring at him.

As Rissa kept walking, Barney felt her heart beating hard but not fast, like a bull against a gate. She was worried. Of course she was. She was walking out of school in the middle of the day. Plus, she had just made one very big enemy in the shape of Miss Whipmire.

And, speaking of the former Siamese cat, she was there now, outside the school. Barney could see her about two hundred metres behind them. She was just a speck from this distance. But she was watching as they walked down the very long and straight row of terraced houses which formed Alfred Street. Or was she?

No.

She wasn't watching them. She was crouching down. *Why?*

Then Barney realized.

Miss Whipmire was crouching next to Pumpkin. She was *telling* the cat something. And now it was the ginger swiper himself who was staring at Barney and Rissa. And he kept staring right up until they turned the corner onto Hitchcock Road. Barney remembered what Pumpkin had told him earlier. '*And, besides, we be 'avin' our orders.*'

'It's all right, little cat, don't be scared,' Rissa was whispering in his ear. 'Miss Whipmire is just a very sad and bitter lady. Most humans aren't like that. You'll see . . .'

Barney realized where they were going. They were heading towards the river, which meant Rissa was planning on taking him to her barge. Which would mean food and drink and safety.

But it was going to be a long walk through the outskirts of town, through quiet streets and empty houses, their occupants out at school and work. About three miles, at least, which, even with Rissa's long legs, would mean an hour or more.

And they weren't safe.

Barney didn't understand exactly *why* they weren't safe, but he sensed danger in the air. Little invisible signals from somewhere, picked up by his whiskers the way aerials pick up the sound of music on a radio.

I've got a bad feeling, he miaowed to Rissa. *The swipers – and Miss Whipmire – are trying to kill me.*

She just patted his head and kept going, probably not realizing they were being watched.

Or followed.

Rissa Gets a Shock

It was odd, how it started.

A bronze and black tabby cat sitting on a low garden wall. Rissa and Barney walked towards it as it turned to look at them, then, once they had passed, Barney realized this was one of the swipers he had encountered this morning.

Sure enough, the cat was now following them. And it wasn't alone. A few steps behind the tabby was Pumpkin.

Rissa, Barney said. *We're being followed.*

But, of course, she didn't understand. She just carried on walking without realizing that there were two – no, three now – actually make that four – no, five – *six*. And what about those three at the back? *Nine* cats, walking in a very serious group, keeping their eyes fixed on Barney.

Then Rissa stopped.

A pelican crossing. She pressed the button and waited.

Meanwhile the cats gathered behind Rissa's heels as ominously as a rain cloud stalking the sun. Barney looked at them, scanning the crowd. There seemed to be twice as many as there had been this morning. Barney saw the one with bat-sized ears and a single-fanged tooth sticking out of its mouth. He remembered this one was called Lyka.

'Why are you doing this?' Barney asked them.

They said nothing.

Rissa carried Barney across the road, and the cats followed.

As they got further and further away from the centre of town the streets became quieter, until there was no one. No cars, no pedestrians, just cats. And more than nine now. About twenty, at least.

Enough for Rissa to turn round.

'Whoa!' said Rissa, and Barney felt a big bass drum of shock beat in her chest before she calmed herself down and realized it was only some cats. But soon she began to freak out as they all started purring loudly, rubbing their heads against the bottom of her legs.

'OK, good cats . . . nice cats . . . I'm just going to go now.'

Barney was confused. Why had these swipers been scared to attack him in front of Rissa earlier but were now perfectly fine about it? Then he remembered Miss Whipmire whispering to Pumpkin. Things began to make sense.

Rissa tried to escape the cats without hurting them, by lifting one of her feet high in the air and attempting to step wide onto the pavement. But the persistent creatures didn't allow this to happen, because as her leg rose at least four of the cats dug their claws into her socks and her skin, trying to weigh her back to the ground.

'Ow!'

Rissa had to literally jump free from the cats, and even then she ended up landing on one of their paws.

'I'm sorry,' she said to the swiper she'd stepped on.

Within moments the cats had started to gather again around Rissa's ankles, clawing at her as if she were a tree.

'Get off! That hurts!'

Another – Lyka – had jumped so high she reached Rissa's hand. Her long claws hooked into her skin, causing enough pain for Rissa to drop Barney onto Pumpkin.

'Wotchit, Lyka, he landed on me blinkin' 'ead.'

Barney scrambled to his feet. Swipers circled.

He realized now that even Rissa couldn't save him. Maybe she would have if she'd known who he really was, but as a cat, well, that was a different issue. Cats attacking cats was just nature and sometimes you had to let nature be. True, she did stamp her feet, but it did nothing to shoo off Pumpkin or his fellow swipers. So Barney ran, as fast as he could, pushing his way past Lyka and the bronze and black tabby. He could hear Pumpkin behind.

'Right, boys, geddim! Can't 'ave 'im escape us this time!'

Barney galloped towards some railings and a front garden full of plants and hiding places. He snuck through the railings and realized he wasn't being followed any more. Hiding amid some rhododendrons, he saw the swipers still on the street, frozen with fear.

'It's him!' gasped Lyka.

'The Terrorcat,' said Pumpkin, gravely.

'He can melt your brain if you stare into his eye!' said the tabby.

'He can stop your heart with one whisker curl!' whimpered another, and the panic quickly spread among the others.

'And your breath with a tail swish!'

'He can make your fur feel wet for the rest of your life!'

'He has his own army of hypnotized rottweilers!'

'He is EVIL!!!'

'I want my mummy . . .'

And they turned and fled with the other street cats as Rissa reluctantly walked away in the other direction and Barney did nothing at all. Just stayed breathlessly still, looking past pretty petals to try and get a glimpse of the Terrorcat.

It was the old silver cat he'd always seen staring out of the window. The one with the stitched-up eye. And even though Barney knew he should have felt scared, he didn't. It was strange. As he watched the cat – a fireside, as Mocha had told him – licking his front paws, he couldn't conjure the slightest trace of fear in his heart. Barney felt, in fact, as though he was watching an old friend. The eye was looking right at Barney, but he didn't feel like his brain was melting. He felt, in fact, something else completely. He felt kindness, or maybe even love.

'Who are you?' Barney whispered, too quietly for the Terrorcat to hear.

The Terrorcat seemed sad, and Barney felt an urge to go over and comfort him. But, still, he knew he had to be cautious. So when the silver cat stood up and walked away, Barney didn't follow. He just waited there until it was out of sight, and then he carefully – and watchfully – slipped back between the railings.

There was a pond-sized puddle on the path. Still water lit by the faint morning sun.

Barney looked into the remnants of yesterday's rain and saw a face he recognized. A cat's face, with a white patch of fur around its left eye.

It was the cat he'd seen on his birthday. The one who'd made him feel dizzy. The one Barney had wished he could be in order not to have to face his mum.

To be a cat . . .

And so it was that, right there, Barney's terrible mistake was confirmed.

A Whisper

He went left. He didn't know why. Left just felt better than right. Instinct. And left *was* better, because he recognized the next street he came to, with its bigger detached houses and sky-high trees. It was where the Primm twins lived, but that's not how Barney knew it. He knew it because it was a street he had been on many times in his life. Because it was on the way to Blandford Library. Where his mum worked.

Where his mum was working *right now*.

He would go there.

Yes.

He would go there and *make* his mum understand. Somehow he would tell her the truth.

Her son was now a cat.

A cat, whom Miss Whipmire, along with half the swipers in Blandford, wanted dead.

Oh, and his dad was alive.

Yes, that really would take quite a bit of explaining.

A giant human appeared miles in front of Barney.

It was one of his mum's friends taking out heavy shopping bags from the boot of her car.

Claire! he shouted. *Claire! Claire! Claire!*

He stood at her ankles. Miaowing. *Worth a shot*, he thought. *After all, Miss Whipmire won't be the only former cat around here . . .*

But it was no good.

Claire didn't even look down as she crossed his path, nearly knocking him out with one of her bags as it swung boiler-sized tins of beans at his head.

Barney kept going, feeling very small indeed.

Walking down the road towards the library was like being in the depths of a valley, with enormous parked cars on one side of him and houses on the other. These houses, like all the houses in Blandford, were suddenly bigger than skyscrapers. It was weird. These were the streets he knew better than any other in the world, yet it might as well have been another planet.

Again he had the feeling that someone was watching him. He turned and saw nothing but a dark brown tail sticking out from behind the wheel of a parked car. The tail quickly whipped away.

Time to speed up, Barney said to himself.

He galloped, cat-style (of course), to the library, turning round every time he heard the tinkling of a collar.

Then, a whisper.

'They're after you,' came a voice.

Barney looked. Couldn't see anything except the wheel of a car.

'What? The swipers?'

'They follow Caramel,' said the same dark brown cat he'd seen behind the car as he walked to the library, who – incidentally – was Mocha's sister, born in the same litter (even if she hadn't seen her sister for seven years). 'She rewards their loyalty with sardines and catnip. In return she gets protection from some of the most deadly swipers in Blandford.'

'Oh,' said Barney, remembering what he had seen outside the school gates. 'You mean Miss Whipmire.'

'They're getting closer. Hide.' And then she darted away. A fast blur of chocolate-brown fur.

Barney only had a short distance to go, across the road and then the bowling green, but he felt exposed, and he panicked, the way he had seen insects panic when he'd turned over stones or lifted up plant pots in his garden.

I'm never going to scare an insect again, he told himself, *if this is how it feels.*

Then it was there.

One of the largest buildings in Blandford, made of

glass like a giant greenhouse. Not the best hiding place in the world, now he thought about it.

There was his mother's Mini in the car park.

He trod through a puddle of old rain and looked up at the steps which led to automatic doors. He doubted he'd be able to get them to open on his own. But then he saw a woman and her little boy arrive, so he waited and snuck in behind them, looking in every direction for his mother.

A City of Books

It was a city of books.

Every aisle between the towering bookshelves was street-sized. The shelves themselves seemed impossibly high, but at least he was unseen here. Barney had deliberately chosen an aisle with no people. He looked up and saw the same label on all the shelves: *Classic Literature. Authors S–Z.*

He saw books with spines as tall and wide as doors, large names on them: *William Shakespeare. Leo Tolstoy. Mark Twain. Voltaire.* Barney had no idea that all four of these very famous dead writers had, at one time or another, been cats. Or that one of them had even admitted to having been a cat. (That one was Mark Twain, who had written very brilliant books about Tom Sawyer and Huckleberry Finn, who were both boys but acted more like wild and adventurous cats, and were based on Mark Twain's own early years as a tomcat. Hence the clue, *Tom* Sawyer.) Indeed, as I think I've told you, most of the really brilliant people who have ever lived have been cats at one time or another. And that is because many of the great cat geniuses, in cat form, get very fed up of not having the kind of wiggly thumbs and fingers that let you write a book.

And you know when people say, 'I just don't know where she (or he) gets it from' – the 'it' meaning imagination or talent or nastiness? You can be pretty sure he (or she) gets it from having been a cat somewhere along the line. Or knowing or loving someone who used to be a cat.

Anyway, I digress. Let's get back to—

Barney.

He was trying to lift his neck as high as possible to look over the lowest row of books. He saw the desk, but there was only a man at it. A man with orange hair and an orange moustache, eating an orange. Barney had seen him before, when he'd been here with his mum. The man was called Jeremy, Barney remembered, and he had been a bit grumpy.

He still looked grumpy now, actually, as he chewed his orange and stared crossly towards a noisy little girl and her mum who were in the far corner looking at picture books.

'BORING!' the girl was yelling as her mum showed her a book about crocodiles. 'Want DVD!'

And she really liked saying 'DVD' so she kept on saying it, as a kind of chant. 'DVD! DVD! DVD!'

Barney turned back round. If he didn't find his mother soon, then someone else was bound to find *him*, and he'd be thrown outside to fend for himself against those evil and obviously super-powered cats.

And there she was!

Three bookshelves along. He could see her jeans. She must have been stacking more books back in place. The trouble was, there was no way of reaching her without stepping out into the view of the orange man. And, anyway, he couldn't just reach his mum with no plan. How could he prove who he was? Then inspiration struck.

He had it!

It was perfect!

And a stroke of luck aided his plan. Barney heard an incredibly loud wail coming from the picture-book section. The little girl was now crying and screaming, throwing books all over the place.

'No like croccy-dile! No like teddy bear! DVD! DVD! DVD!'

Her mother – a blonde lady wearing a lot of make-up – was crouching over her, hands hovering nervously, as though her daughter was a very dangerous and complicated bomb.

'Calm down, Florence. It's all right. Come on, sweetheart. Let's go home and watch a DVD. You can watch *Princess Piglet*. That's your favourite. And you can have some jelly stars too!'

'No want jeh-wee stars! Want choc-lutt! CHOC-LUTT!'

'You can have some chocolate. Just, please . . . get off the floor.'

'No, Mummy! No! No-aaaaagh!'

Meanwhile orange man, Jeremy, had finished eating his fruit and was now stepping out from behind the desk to walk over and get cross with the little girl in pink and her mother.

So, this was the moment.

Barney ran, fast and low, feeling yet again like a panicking ant, down the aisle, over a book that had fallen off the shelf with the words: Shakespeare, *A Midsummer Night's Dream* on the cover. Then he reached his mum. Staring up at her face, he realized she looked worried. What he didn't know was that she had already heard the message Rissa had left this morning by using her mobile to check her home answering machine. But Rissa hadn't said much. She'd been cut off, so Mrs Willow didn't have a clue what it had been about.

Barney's mum had tried phoning back but there was no answer. So she had then phoned the school, and the secretary had put her through to Miss Whip-mire herself (who Barney's mum hadn't even asked to speak to).

'Oh, yes, don't worry,' Miss Whipmire had said in a most reassuring voice. 'He's at school. I just saw him only a moment ago. But I'm afraid he will be very late home as he got into a bit of trouble in the school corridor.'

'Trouble?'

'Yes. Bullying. Picking on other Year Sevens.'

'*Bullying?* That doesn't sound like Barney.'

And Miss Whipmire had laughed. 'What? After the fire alarm?'

'Fire alarm? What fire alarm?'

'Listen, no mother ever likes to believe their son could be a little monster. But let me assure you, he's been a little monster these past two days. I've seen it with my own eyes . . . So I've had no choice but to give him a detention. He won't be home until eight o'clock tonight.'

'Eight? A four-hour detention? That seems a bit excessive.'

'Excessive deeds require excessive measures, Mrs Willow.'

It had been a strange conversation. And it was the reason why she looked troubled as Barney miaowed up at her.

Mum. Look. Down here. Look at me.

And she did look, as she slipped a thin book of poetry onto a high shelf.

'It's *you*,' she said.

She recognized him! But then Barney's heart sank as she said, 'The cat from this morning. What are *you* doing here? Come on . . . no cats are allowed in the library.'

Barney waited for his mum to reach down for him and, at the last available moment, sprang away from her, wanting her to follow. He looked up at the sides of the bookshelves until he was where he wanted to be.

Classics: A–K.

He ran along, looking desperately at the spines of books.

Jane Austen, *Pride and Prejudice* . . . Emily Brontë, *Wuthering Heights* . . . Samuel Taylor Coleridge, *The Rime of the Ancient Mariner* . . .

Then he got there. To the Ks.

His plan was to find his favourite book, *The Water Babies* by Charles Kingsley. It was an old book that he had found one evening and which hadn't been taken out of the library since 22 August 1982. It was a bit of an odd story really, about a boy who falls into a pond and turns into a weird creature called a Water Baby. Anyway, Barney liked it, odd or not, and he'd read it

178

about ten times when his parents first divorced. Plus a few times since.

And his mum knew he liked it because he had kept asking her to get it out for him again and again. So he thought that if he deliberately went over to that book and touched it with his paws, even tried to pull it off the shelf, then he might just get her to realize he was her son. And he knew the book would be on the bottom shelf because that was where it always was.

Trouble was, *The Water Babies* was nowhere to be seen, which was very weird because Barney was sure he was the only person who ever took it out of the library. Well, since 1982, anyway. So Barney looked for another book that he liked, but he couldn't see any except *The Jungle Book* by Rudyard Kipling, which he hadn't actually really liked very much but which was at least a book his mum knew he'd read. It was on the third shelf so he tried to jump. But Barney couldn't get anywhere near where he wanted to be. All he did was bring down another book. A hardback which fell on top of him. He could see the cover, with the scary-looking block capitals KAFKA and METAMORPHOSIS falling towards him, before the inevitable clunk on the head.

So, his plan had failed.

Barney hadn't been able to look like anything but an insane cat, and now his mother's hands were on his ribs, trying to pull him off the carpet his claws didn't want to leave.

She carried him – past all the books made specifically for human hands, books he knew he might never have the chance to read again. And now there was someone else.

Jeremy.

The orange man.

'What is *that* doing in here?' he asked, disgusted.

'No idea,' said Barney's mum. 'Believe it or not, I'm pretty sure this is the same cat I saw in my house this morning. You know, the one I was telling you about.'

'Odd,' said Jeremy. 'Oh well. This isn't a zoo.'

He pointed to the automatic doors, meaning for Barney's mum to throw him out of the library. And she would have done if it hadn't been for the little girl in pink. The one who had been screaming 'DVD' moments before.

Florence.

'Mummy, look! Look, Mummy! LOOK NOW!'

Her mummy looked.

'Oh, gosh! It's Maurice.'

Maurice?

Who was Maurice?

Barney saw them both walk over, and the woman tell his mum and Jeremy that the cat belonged to them.

'How can we be sure the cat's yours?' asked Jeremy suspiciously.

Florence's mum got out her phone, and moments later showed them a picture of a black cat with a white patch of fur around its left eye. To Barney's horror, the cat was dressed in a fairy costume, complete with wings, and looked very uncomfortable.

'Wan' go home!' Florence was wailing. 'Wan' go home an' see Gaff-Gaff!'

'There you go,' said Mrs Willow, handing her son over to a complete stranger.

Mum. It's me.

For the one thousandth time.

Barney saw the automatic doors slide behind him and his mum standing inside the library, watching him leave.

I love you, he said, because it seemed like a very long time since he had told her that, and because he didn't know if he would get the opportunity again.

Not that it meant anything.

It was just another faint miaow, lost on the breeze.

The Cattery

Hi. It's the author again. Now, I know what you're wondering. You're wondering, *Hey, what happened to that cat you mentioned nearly a hundred pages ago? Mocha, or whatever her name was.*

Oh? You're not wondering that? Oh dear, that author M-RMR (Mind-Reading My Readers) kit my mum bought me for Christmas must be going a bit faulty. Never mind, I'll tell you about Mocha, anyway, because by telling you about her I'll really be telling you about something much more important.

She was there in her cage in the cattery. By 'cage', I mean a soft, warm room with a giant sheepskin rug for a carpet and a view of rolling meadows out of the window. And by 'cattery' I mean swank palace. Seriously, Edgarton Cattery was like the poshest hotel you've ever been to. Only better. Well, if you were a cat you'd think it was better. Because of the toys and stuff. Fluffy mice, scratch posts, litter trays – which instead of that uncomfortable gravelly stuff had a picture of a dog for the cats to look at as they toileted all over said canine's poor poochy face.

Right now, Mocha was enjoying a late lunch. Grilled sardines coupled with battered field mouse and washed down with a saucer of double cream. Of course, the company could have been a bit better. It wasn't much fun listening to the cats on either side of her. One, a no-hoper who was now an old tabby called Tiddles but had once been a human chartered accountant called Peter Michael Thimblethwaite, kept on moaning about how he'd visited Blandford Golf Course to visit his brother but hadn't been recognized. 'He had me kicked me off the blinking course! He wouldn't even be a member if it wasn't for me!'

The cat in the other neighbouring cage was a fireside called Elton – a fluffy white Persian moaning about his early retirement.

'I used to be a calendar cat, you know . . . Oh yes, humans used to take photos of me sprawled out on the grass in the sunshine . . . My face adorns over a million walls, you know . . . Well, for one month of the year . . . But now I'm too old apparently . . . My fur's all tired and matted . . . My eyes have lost their twinkle . . . And Persians are out of fashion, they say . . . "Your look is too opulent . . . It is too

1980s . . . We want scruffy-looking cats . . ." And they do! Have you seen the models recently? They have *swipers* now . . . Seriously, where has all the *class* gone? It's all filth and fleas! Filth and fleas!'

Elton went on like this for hours. But Mocha didn't mind, and concentrated her thoughts elsewhere, such as on the tall human girl talking to the cattery owner, who the cats knew only as the Man of Infinite Kindness. A man who every cat seemed to feel affection for, without understanding why.

She was there, this human girl, leaning over the desk and staring into the man's face. Mocha had seen this human girl before. She had walked by Mocha's house once with Barney Willow. And now she was talking urgently to the Man of Infinite Kindness.

'But you look *exactly* like him,' the girl was saying, getting nothing but an awkward glance in response. 'So . . . what is your name then if it's not Mr Neil Willow?'

'It's Smith.'

'Just Smith?'

'Please, I've got a lot of things to do . . .'

Mocha watched the Man of Infinite Kindness type something on his computer, trying to look busy. But there was no stopping the tall girl with the crazy hair.

'Your son is worried about you. He thinks you might be dead . . . I'm Rissa. Rissa Fairweather. I'm Barney's best friend.'

'I'm not him.'

'But you sound like him. You look like him. Barney's . . . Barney's missing. I think he might have come to look for you.'

'There has been no boy here, I assure you . . .'

Rissa was trying not to get angry. 'Well maybe you could help us. Maybe if you made a public announcement and told local TV that you'd come back, or something.'

The Man of Infinite Kindness was also the Man of Infinite Patience, Mocha realized. He just sighed thoughtfully and seemed genuinely worried for the girl. 'Listen, the boy you are looking for might not be missing.'

'What? Of course he is.'

'He might have come to you but you didn't recognize him. Trust me, keep your mind open to the impossible and you will find the truth.'

Rissa had no idea what he was talking about. 'Look, if you see him will you contact me?' She handed over a crumpled piece of paper.

And then he looked at Rissa with eyes that were

as honest as eyes can look. 'Of course.'

Rissa looked uncertain, but just at that moment a woman came in carrying a Burmese cat called Lapsang, who Mocha knew from the fences. 'Hello, I'm Mrs Hunter,' the woman said. 'I've booked Lapsang in for two weeks . . . We've heard ever such good things about this cattery.'

The Man of Infinite Kindness smiled softly, pretending Rissa wasn't still there. 'Well, I just try and make cats as comfortable as they can be.'

Lapsang, meanwhile, was looking all around over Mrs Hunter's shoulder, miaowing in pleasure. 'Now *this* is more like it. Oh, Mocha, sweetie darling, I didn't see you there.' Then Lapsang spied someone else, a grizzled and rather scruffy-looking moggy in a cage near the entrance. His ear was damaged, bitten. 'Oooh,' she mewed in disgust. 'A *swiper*.'

'That's low,' grumbled the moggy. 'I'm a rescue cat, posh-paws, there's a difference . . .'

But Mocha stayed watching Rissa. The girl was looking confused and a bit defeated as she backed away out of the cattery, wondering what was best for her friend.

Over The Hill From Weird

Rissa caught a bus home.

'*This isn't just weird,*' she told herself. '*This is over the hill from weird.*'

She stared out of the window at the fast-moving houses. She knew that the man had looked very much like Barney's dad, but at the same time there was something that wasn't right. When she had looked into his eyes she had felt, very surely, that she had been looking into the eyes of a stranger.

Again, all this weirdness was making her more worried about Barney. She got off at the closest stop to home, walked through the streets, along the river path to her parents' barge. She stepped inside, crouching as she went down the little wooden steps to the galley and then the narrow living quarters beyond.

Her mum and dad weren't there.

Rissa went to the small fridge, which was old and battered and had a big sticker of a rainbow on it.

She opened it up and saw some of her mum's special carrot cake. Normally she couldn't get enough of the stuff, but today she realized she wouldn't be able to eat anything, even though she'd left most of her pizza at lunch.

She went to her bedroom. *Bedroom* wasn't really the word for it. It was more like a narrow box, with a tiny porthole and a futon instead of a bed, and a beanbag instead of a chair. But Rissa liked it. The sound of the water lapping against the bow of the boat usually made her feel very calm.

Usually.

Not today, though.

On the floor by her futon was a book her dad had taken out of the library especially for her. It was a book Barney had always gone on about and she'd wanted to try herself.

The Water Babies, by Charles Kingsley.

She'd started it last night, and had decided she didn't like the way the boy character was so perfect and the girl was so horrible. But she did like the way the writer had made water so magical. Looking out of her porthole at night and seeing the moonlight reflected on the surface of the river was enough to make you believe life was full of a million unfathomable wonders. It was the same feeling Rissa had when looking through her telescope at stars that had died millions of years ago, even though their light lives on.

She stared at the book. And then it came to her. Of course. The *library*.

She phoned it, asked to speak to Mrs Willow.

'Oh, Rissa. Hello. What's wrong?'

Rissa thought about telling Barney's mum about her visit to the cattery, but she really didn't know what to say. Had she seen Mr Willow or hadn't she? So instead she said: 'It's Barney.'

'Barney? I phoned the school earlier and spoke to Miss Whipmire. She told me he's fine. He's at school. But he's been a bit badly behaved.'

Rissa waited a moment. This didn't make sense. 'No,' she said. 'He's not been at school today. He ran away. I tried to tell you in my message but the bus driver took the phone off me.'

A pause. Rissa heard Mrs Willow's anxious breath creating a fuzzy noise on the phone. 'Miss Whipmire assured me he was there.'

'Well,' said Rissa, not knowing how else to put this, 'I'm afraid that Miss Whipmire is a liar.'

Princess Piglet's Pink and Pretty Perfectly Perfect Princess Party (and Other Forms of Torture)

It would have been a massive house even by human standards, but from a cat-sized perspective it was like entering the largest palace you could imagine.

Everything was cream-coloured. The carpets, the walls, the lampshade, the sofa in the front room. It was there that Barney was now sitting watching the seventeenth episode of *Princess Piglet* in a row ('Princess Piglet's Pink and Pretty Perfectly Perfect Princess Party'). That would have been torture enough, even without Florence trying to poke his eyes between episodes and holding him so tight to her he could hardly breathe.

Florence's mummy came in after a bit. 'Oh, come on, Florence, leave that poor cat alone,' she said, and to Barney's relief rescued him from the little girl's hands.

'No, Mummy! Want cat! Want cat eyes! Like 'weeties.'

'Florence,' said her mother calmly. 'Cats' eyes aren't sweeties. And neither are dogs' eyes. Poor Leonard. Honestly, you and your brother!' And then she looked down at Barney. 'No wonder you ran away, is it, Maurice?'

Oh, no, thought Barney.

Florence had a brother.

A brother, who, by the sound of things, was just as bad as Florence.

Who between them (and possibly the dog) had caused him – or Maurice, rather – to run away.

He'd *run away*.

Well, obviously *they* thought that. But it was impossible for Barney to know if that was true. The cat had left his house and had bumped into Barney after he'd ripped up Miss Whipmire's letter. But had the cat actually run away? Florence's mum thought he had because she hadn't seen him, but she hadn't seen him because he'd become a human, and because Barney had become him – Maurice. And if there was a way of getting back into his own body then Maurice, the Barney-Who-Wasn't-Barney, would know.

As he was placed back down on the carpet Barney had a thought. A tantalizing and brilliant thought.

Maybe Maurice had come home.

And so Barney went out of the room to search the enormous house for signs of his human body.

But it wasn't any good. There was furniture – a *lot* of furniture – but nothing else. He couldn't find himself anywhere on the ground floor. But in the kitchen, next to the cat basket, he found something quite worrying.

A larger basket with a faded, smelly tartan blanket creeping out onto the floor.

The *dog's* basket. And a big dog, judging by the size of it.

Barney looked around for an escape route. He saw one.

A cat flap next to the fridge.

Locked.

His heart sank, anchored, then lifted again.

He stared at the food Florence's mum had put out for him. Jellied meat shone from the small bowl, looking almost as disgusting as it smelled.

Then a thought.

Dogs talk cat.

Cats talk dog.

And not all dogs were Guster.

With this in mind Barney decided to go upstairs for answers. But upstairs didn't have answers. It just had a carpet which made him sneeze, a bathroom with a very slippy floor, and lots of toys lying about everywhere.

Giant baby dolls, mutilated teddy bears, armless Barbies. As he walked along the landing, Barney felt like he was surveying a battlefield after a completely one-sided war.

He spotted four bedrooms. There was the one with a neatly made double bed and a picture of Florence's mum with a man who Barney guessed was probably Florence's dad. It reminded Barney of the photo of his mum and dad on holiday in the south of France. A photo that Mum ripped up during the divorce and then stuck back together after his dad went missing. There was another photo too, of Florence and her brother. Barney couldn't see it very well as it was high up on a chest and, plus, the sun was streaming in through the window reflecting on the glass into the frame; still, he was sure he recognized the brother from somewhere.

Florence's room had even more wounded toys than the hallway. There was a toy ambulance, which was very appropriate, lots of plastic farm animals and *Princess Piglet* characters, along with a giant, over-stretched stethoscope.

The next bedroom was a spare one and looked empty, so Barney didn't bother exploring. But opposite was a near-closed door. *Must be the brother's bedroom.*

The toxic smell of stale socks and spray-on deodorant wafted towards him, making his whiskers curl in disgust.

Barney felt prickly with nerves as he entered, although at first he saw nothing too worrying. Just posters of cars and shelves of video games. He looked at some of the titles.

Endless Warfare IV: Total Destruction
Alien Apocalypse
Joe Hero and the Land of
Endless Violence

As he looked around the room – at the football on the floor, at the giant TV and brand-new computer, at the rugby jersey over the back of a chair – he had a very troubled feeling.

He remembered what Florence had said.

Gaff-Gaff.

He looked at the door.

There was a sticker on it which said:

> GOVERNMENT WARNING – THIS ROOM CONTAINS
>
> TRACES OF
>
> Gavin
>
> ENTER AT YOUR OWN RISK!

Downstairs, a phone rang.

Florence's mum answered. 'Yes, I'm Mrs Needle . . . How can I help you?'

Needle.

Gavin.

Needle.

No.

No no no no *no*.

And, yet, it made terrible sense. It certainly explained Florence's evil-ness. She was a Needle! Gavin's little sister.

Marmalade, he told himself. But that only made him think of Rissa and reminded him he was all alone. *How ungrateful I've been!* he thought. *OK, I didn't have a dad. But I had Rissa. I had Mum. That made me twice as lucky as I am now.*

He noticed, after he'd thought this, that some fur from his face and neck had dropped down onto the carpet forming a little cloud of black hairs.

Miss Whipmire's Visitor

Barney's mum had only met Miss Whipmire once before. It had been after Barney had got in trouble for causing disruption in a school assembly.

She had believed her then.

But now, in Miss Whipmire's office, she wasn't sure what she believed.

'Yes, Mrs Willow, what can I do for you?' This was strange. Miss Whipmire hadn't turned from the window she was staring out of, a window which offered a view of a grim February sky and green playing fields where Year Ten girls were engaged in a rather shouty game of hockey. There was no reflection in the glass. And yet she had known precisely who had been knocking on the door.

'Erm, hello . . . yes, it's me. Barney's mum. Elaine. I was just a bit confused about something.'

Miss Whipmire turned sharply. 'Confused? I don't understand.'

Mrs Willow sniffed the air and realized she was

smelling fish. Sardines, she would have guessed. 'Well, it's just – Barney. I've been told by a good friend of his that he's not been in school today,' she said, noticing a very ugly-looking pen pot on the desk. 'So I don't mean to contradict you but I think you might have made a mistake.'

Miss Whipmire said nothing as her face tried on various emotions. First shock, then anger, moving up to full outrage, simmering down to general crossness, then thoughtfulness, then concern, before squeezing uncomfortably into shame.

'Oh, I'm sorry,' she said, as innocent as a lamb at a christening. 'I hope I haven't made a terrible mistake . . . I'll tell you what, I'll just go and have a word with his form tutor.'

Miss Whipmire left the room and Barney's mum waited, staring at the head teacher's calendar. 'Cats,' she whispered aloud, noting the strange theme of her day.

But Miss Whipmire wasn't going to see Mrs Lavender. She was looking out of the school entrance to see if there was any word from her cat disciples.

She could see Pumpkin sitting on the wall opposite looking ashamed of himself. And so he should, the flea-brained cretin.

Barney was still out there, realized Miss Whipmire. *Twice those useless swipers have failed me.*

He was alive and trying to become human again, and then in all probability would attempt to tell the world – or at least the school governors – the truth about her.

But she had a plan. And it was so good that it shone in her mind like an oil-sleek sardine in a can. And, with that plan in her mind, she headed out of the school gates to have a word with her chief disciple.

A Bit About Pumpkin

Miss Whipmire crossed over the road to talk to Pumpkin.

By the way, in case you are one of those readers who has to know everything about every single character in a book, I'll tell you a few facts about this particular swiper. He was stupid. Stupid enough to do anything Miss Whipmire asked of him. He had known her when she'd been a Siamese cat, and hadn't liked her very much as she had been a fireside, and firesides and swipers are never the best of friends. Plus, she had been critical of his fence-walking skills. But she had been a good fighter, and good fighting always impressed Pumpkin, especially if the fighting was being done by a fireside. And then, after she had become a human, he was even more impressed. It was useful having friends in human places, especially ones who made sure he was stocked up on sardines in lemon-infused olive oil, his absolute favourite. (Even the roughest of swipers has sophisticated taste when it comes to fish.) And it gave him kudos out on the street to be a TLC's favourite. (TLC: Two-Legged Cat. Street slang for cats-turned-into-humans. The opposite of a no-hoper, which I believe has been mentioned – human-turned-cat.) Not that Pumpkin ever wanted to be a TLC himself. No. He was perfectly happy being an orange moggy, cruising gardens, networking, boxing flies, rubbing up against old ladies in exchange for milk, and flirting with Lyka (who was never interested).

Where was I?

Oh yes. Somewhere around:

Miss Whipmire crossing over the road to talk to Pumpkin.

He saw her coming and knew she'd be even more cross with him now after his second failed attempt to get the Barney cat. So he was there, ready with an excuse.

'Look, all right . . . OK, thing is, old gal, we failed you,' he said. 'We did. I did. *I* failed you. But there was nothing we could be doing. The Terrorcat showed up. He was going to start using his powers so we had to run . . .'

Pumpkin, by the way, was a succinct cat, and fitted all of the above words into one and a half miaows plus an ear scratch.

Miss Whipmire had no time for chit-chat. 'Get Maurice,' she said. 'And tell him to come to my office.'

Pumpkin was confused. 'But I thought you said you wanted 'im to stay indoors at your 'ouse till the Barney cat was dead.'

Miss Whipmire glared down furiously, for once not caring if anyone could see her through the staff-room window.

'Well, Barney *would* be dead, wouldn't he, if you weren't such an idiot? And, just so you know, if I wanted questions I'd have hired someone with a pedigree,'

she hissed, her nails tingling as if they'd forgotten they weren't claws. 'I need Maurice here because I happen to have Mrs Willow in my office, wondering where her son is. Now do it. *Go.*'

Pumpkin went.

She looked up and saw a girl in Year Ten staring at her as she shouted at the cat. 'And what are you doing out of school, girl?' Miss Whipmire snapped.

'School's over, miss. I was just coming back for choir practice.'

'Oh yes, you're the terrible singer. Are you wearing make-up?'

'No.'

'Well, you should. Or just try a paper bag. No eye-holes. You look hideous.'

And, as the girl ran crying into the school, Miss Whipmire sighed to herself in disgust. '*Humans.*'

An Accurate Description

'Your son will be here shortly,' Miss Whipmire said, on her return to the office. 'He's just, erm, playing an important game of rugby right now.'

'*Really?*' said Mrs Willow, looking out of the window at the girls playing hockey. 'I didn't think he had games today.'

The head teacher drew the blinds closed then sat down on her chair, smoothing her back against the sheepskin rug.

'Well, don't worry. As I say, he's on his way.'

They chit-chatted a while, then sat in silence for almost half an hour.

Miss Whipmire sensed Barney's mum was feeling horribly awkward sitting in that room, which made her happy.

'Are you a cat person, Mrs Willow?'

'Erm, no. Not really.'

A condescending smile. 'Didn't think so.'

'Oh, right.'

'I've lost my cat.'

'Really? Oh.'

'Yes,' said Miss Whipmire, acting every bit the concerned pet owner. 'He's called Patch. Because of the white patch of fur around his left eye.'

'How weird. I've just seen a cat like that.'

I bet you have, thought Miss Whipmire. 'Really?'

'Yes. But this one belonged to someone else. A woman saw it and claimed it after it came into the library.'

'Oh?' Then Miss Whipmire's face screwed up with false pain. 'Oh, please, oh, no, don't tell me it "belonged" to a lady with blonde hair, wearing a bit too much make-up and over-sized earrings.'

Barney's mum thought, and her face revealed that this was a pretty accurate description. 'Well, *yes*.'

'So my dear little Patch is with her?'

'She said the cat's name was Maurice.'

Miss Whipmire wanted to try and make Barney's mum feel guilty, just for fun, but she decided not to. She had all the information she needed, and making too big a deal out of it would only arouse suspicion. And the suspicion had to wait at least until Barney Willow was dead.

She smiled. 'Oh, don't worry. I'm sure it was a totally different cat.'

And around about then there came a knock on the door.

'Come in,' said Miss Whipmire.

A boy who looked every bit like Barney entered. Mrs Willow stood up and hugged him. 'I've been so worried about you!'

'See, I told you he was OK, Mrs Willow. And, look, he's all red and sweaty from playing rugby.'

Maurice realized this was his cue. 'Yes, Mum, I've been playing rugby.'

'Now,' said Miss Whipmire in a rather clipped tone, 'if you don't mind, I've really got quite a lot of business to attend to. You'll see Barney later on. Don't worry.'

And so Mrs Willow left, mildly confused but generally relieved, and headed outside to her car. Inside the office, meanwhile, Miss Whipmire was touching Maurice's face.

Her son's face.

'Oh, my darling, you've done it! You've done it! My brilliant, brilliant boy!'

And Maurice smiled softly. He was pleased to see

his mum, and happy not to belong to the Needles, but he still wasn't comfortable yet in his new skin. 'Yeah. I love you, Mum.'

His mother didn't hear him as his words coincided with the sound of the bell ringing for the final time that day.

'Now, listen,' she said. 'Here's the plan.'

The Warney Pillow

Barney gazed around the room with that weird kind of excited terror that comes from being in an enemy's territory when the enemy isn't around. He was about to leave when he saw something lying on the bed. Something soft and grey and sad-looking. A donkey! *Eeyore!* Gavin Needle had a cuddly Eeyore on his bed.

For a moment this struck Barney as such a brilliant piece of information that he forgot about being a cat. But he was reminded when he heard a noise. The kind of noise that when you are a cat you can't really ignore.

It wasn't loud.

Just a whimper, really, coming from somewhere else.

The dog.

Leonard.

Barney waited.

It would have been perfectly easy for him to sneak out of the room and run back downstairs, but Barney reminded himself he'd come upstairs for answers.

So, with a determination he felt speed his heart and flick his tail, he went out and followed the sound all the way to the spare room.

This is crazy.

What kind of cat seeks out a dog?

He crossed the carpet, and detected the faint but rather putrid smell of sweating dog. A pair of wide, bulging brown eyes stared out from under the bed. A giant skinny monster of black and brown fur. A Doberman. Barney tried not to panic.

'Hello,' said Barney. 'I'm Barney.'

'What?' Leonard sounded nervous and actually rather desperate. 'You've forgotten your own name. Or . . . or . . .'

'No. I haven't. It's just I'm not who you think I am . . . I'm not Maurice.'

'I'm going mad! First the cushions and now this.'

Barney didn't understand. 'The cushions?'

'Yes, they've turned against me. The ones on the bed. They're always *frowning* at me. Trying to make me feel weird. Look! Are they still there?'

Barney stepped back, and checked on top of the bed. There were indeed cushions. Two of them. Normal square cushions crumpled on the bed.

'I don't think they're *frowning*,' Barney said, trying

to reassure the frightened dog. 'I just think they're creased.'

'Creased? That's what they want you to think.'

Barney started to back away. Leonard was obviously too mad to be of any help.

'Don't leave me again,' he drooled. '*Please.*'

Barney hesitated. 'I'm sorry but I don't belong here. I have my own home.' He turned, was nearly at the door.

'Don't go to the Whipmires',' implored Leonard.

'What?'

The dog wasn't listening. 'I told the radiator earlier. I said, "That's all he used to talk about, Mummy-Caramel-Whipmire-Mummy-Caramel-Whipmire."'

'Did you just say Caramel?'

'I had a job!' the dog said, adding to Barney's confusion.

'*What?*'

The dog clenched his eyes shut. 'I was a somebody! I worked in security! But do I ever think of going back?! Do I? No! Yes! No! No! Yes! But I don't. I can't. The cushions won't let me. And even if they did, I wouldn't, because I have different owners now. And I accept that.' Right then he looked more sad than mad. 'I have to accept that.'

'Listen, please, you have to help me,' said Barney, trying to sound as gentle and soothing as possible.

The dog ignored him, and recited a slow, sad piece of Doberman poetry.

'Oh, who can love a dog like me?
Not the cute one on TV
With golden hair for all to stroke,
And who fails to see life's big joke.

No, I am not a Labrador,
Or a terrier with tiny paws,
No, I'm not one you hug and squeeze,
Or that lies flat out upon your knees.

I'm a different kind of breed,
One in which you can't succeed,
Unless you are prepared to scare
The ones you want to love and care.'

The Doberman seemed far away, lost in his own sad, mad thoughts.

But Barney had an idea. 'Listen, please, you've got to help me. The . . . erm, *cushions* say you've got to help me.'

The Doberman switched to alert mode. '*What?*

215

They said that?'

'Yes,' Barney insisted, thinking on his paws. 'They said you have to tell me what you know about Maurice. They want you to tell me why you think he ran away?'

'To see his mummy,' said the dog, chewing at his front paw. 'He wants to see his mummy. As if we don't all want to see our mummies!'

'Caramel?'

'Caramel! Caramel! Caramel! All day long. Caramel . . .'

Barney thought. *Caramel. Miss Whipmire.* 'Maurice is Miss Whipmire's son!'

The dog studied him. For a moment Barney could imagine Leonard's former self: the responsible guard dog. 'Someone came one day. A ginger cat. He had a message.'

'What was the message?'

'I don't know. It was a whispered message. All I know is that Maurice was never the same again. He said he was going to escape. He was going to find a pillow.'

'A *pillow*?'

'Or a Billow. The Warney Billow or Pillow. And that would somehow make everything all right.'

Warney Billow.

Barney Willow.

Barney realized that cat hadn't been there by accident yesterday afternoon. 'So, it was all deliberate. He targeted me on purpose. But why *me*?'

'I don't know. Please, tell the cushions I'm sorry.'

'They'll . . . get over it,' Barney said. 'They look like very understanding cushions.'

And Barney stepped backwards, away from those crazed eyes under the bed, and retreated out of the room, realizing that whatever had been whispered in that message would explain everything. Then he remembered something Miss Whipmire had said as she'd waved that envelope with her address on it. '*These are my tickets. Mine and my only love's. Out of here for ever. This time tomorrow I'll be en route to Old Siam – Thailand.*'

If Barney was to find Maurice, he now knew where to start – he'd need to pay a visit to Miss Whipmire's house. But he also knew he didn't have long before his human self was on a plane to the other side of the world.

Then Barney's heart sank further as he heard the front door open and close, and Florence squeal with delight. 'Gaff-Gaff home! Gaff-Gaff home!'

Toilet Trouble

Gavin had been home for five minutes, and for three of those minutes he had been standing on Barney's tail.

Barney had hidden in the bathroom. Trouble was, Gavin always needed the toilet when he came home from school, and he'd managed to shut the door before Barney could escape.

And now the boy was sitting on the toilet, trousers around his ankles, and the sole of his left shoe (more of a boot) was pressing hard enough into Barney's tail bone to cause the kind of pain that makes you think fondly of being crushed on a rugby pitch.

'*Ow*,' Barney was saying. (The one word that is the same in both cat and human.)

'Sorry?' Gavin was saying as he laughed. 'What's the matter, Maurice?'

Please get off my tail.

'No idea what you're talking about.'

Yes you do, you evil psycho. Please. It hurts.

And Gavin stared down into Maurice's face. 'You look different. Wimpier. You look like . . .' He shook his head, as if dismissing a silly thought. 'Anyway, what were you doing at the bus stop this morning? I don't want my cat following me to school. Makes me look soft. And I don't like looking soft. Because I'm Gavin. And Gavin's the Greek word for rock.' (It's not, by the way, Gavin was just an idiot.) 'And that's what I am. I am a big rock.'

I could think of some other words, wailed Barney.

'So, don't do it again, fur-face, or you're dead,' continued Gavin. 'Understand me? D. E. D. *Dead.*'

D. E. A. D., actually, said Barney.

Gavin didn't know he was being taunted by his cat, but pressed harder on his tail anyway, just for fun. So it was a sweet relief when the doorbell rang downstairs and the pressure lifted.

'Who's that?' wondered Gavin aloud as he tore off a very long sheet of toilet paper.

Then: 'Gavin! *Gavin?!* Could you get that? I'm on my exercise bike.'

'Yuh,' said Gavin, in caveman.

Gavin finished up and went downstairs, and Barney sped after him, close to his heels. Gavin opened the door. 'Hello,' said a man selling cloths and feather

219

dusters. 'Could I speak to the home owner, young man?'

Barney never heard Gavin's reply. He was out. And he was running. Because he knew he couldn't waste a second.

63 Sycamore Terrace

Sycamore Terrace was the most normal-looking street you have ever seen. It was so normal-looking that even if you had never been on it before you would think you had, because it was like so many other streets you've been on. It had normal-looking houses. The houses had normal-looking doors and windows. True, there was one piece of graffiti, on a wall near the end of the road, but the street was so boringly normal and uninspiring that the graffiti just said, 'Graffiti'. And the most absolutely normal thing of all was the house at number 63.

Sandwiched in a terrace between the still-pretty-average 61 and 65 – where the Freeman children had once lived (the ones who had blown away a certain cat's tail with a firework) – number 63 was so achingly normal it made its otherwise bland neighbouring houses look positively crazy with their patterned curtains and Neighbourhood Watch window stickers. Seriously, number 63 was so boring-looking, with its door and its three windows and its roof, that you could forget what it looked like *even as you looked at it.*

But as Barney arrived outside in the fading evening light he felt anything but bored. After all, he knew who lived at this house. And he knew that if he had a chance of becoming his true self again then this was the most obvious place to start looking.

He was relieved to see no sign of Miss Whipmire's silver car. It was Wednesday evening. The weekly school governors' meeting. This was good. Hopefully he'd be able to go inside, find Maurice and be out by the time she came back.

Barney went through the passageway between 63 and 65, under the wooden gate.

'Wait, cat,' mumbled a kind-hearted woodlouse clinging upside down to the damp wood. 'It's dangerous in there.'

'Thanks,' said Barney, but ignored the advice. He crossed the back yard, noticing the smell of fish getting stronger as he approached the cat flap in the back door. The cat flap was transparent plastic but it was too clouded to see what was inside. Before he pushed his head through, Barney had a quick look at the garden. It was considerably overgrown, the lawn didn't look like it had been mown for years, and the flower beds were full of weeds. By the back wall of the house leaned the real Miss Whipmire's old bicycle, now unused and covered in rust. Barney realized that the sleek silver car that Miss Whipmire now drove must have been purchased after the head teacher and her cat had swapped places.

Barney pressed his way inside. He was in the kitchen, and at first he could think of nothing but the smell. Fishy smells filled his nostrils and wet his tongue. And he could see why. The kitchen was full of fish. The kitchen table was covered in fresh silver trout. There were open tins of pilchards and tuna on the scruffy units, and a pile of unopened sardine tins. And all around the floor there were fish bones – complete skeletons, sometimes, with the heads still untouched. Barney crossed through as quietly as he could, trying to ignore the dead trout eyes staring blankly up at him.

Then he heard a voice.

'Excuse me!' it squeaked. 'I appear to be a little bit stuck.'

Barney followed the voice and reached a wooden board, on which was fastened a brown mouse trapped beneath a thin rod of metal. A mousetrap.

'Sorry . . .' The mouse could hardly breathe. The metal was digging fast into his neck, only minutes away from slicing his head clean off. 'I don't make a habit of asking cats for help, of course. And I wouldn't mind, really. I mean, my life's not been much to write home about. But I've got little ones who depend on me. I . . . I smelled the cheese and I couldn't help it, it's *gorgonzola* . . .'

Barney didn't know what to do. If he'd still been a human it would have been one thing. But with paws, diminished size and feeble strength it was quite another. Barney noticed a jar of fish oil sitting nearby, knocked it on its side so that it poured over the mouse and the trap, then tried his best to pull back on the metal with one paw while pressing down on the wood with another. With the oil making things slippery, the mouse managed to slide his head out and free as the trap slammed against the wood, taking a few whiskers with it.

'Most rare,' he said, confused, as blood leaked from his neck. 'What kind of cat are you? Saving a humble little mouse like old Moosh here.'

'Actually, I'm a—'

Moosh the mouse suddenly looked terrified and scuttled back to a tiny hole in the skirting board, dripping neck blood and fish oil as he went.

'Wait,' said Barney. 'Where are you go—?'

'Run for your life, kind cat!'

Barney heard the cat flap.

It was the cat with bat-sized ears. Lyka.

Barney quickly ran to the hallway, then upstairs. There were dead fish and their bones up there too, along with bowls of creamy milk lining the landing. He heard a noise downstairs. Then another one, from somewhere upstairs. The sound of a yawn. Someone was waking up. Barney didn't know whether he should be hiding or looking for Maurice. After all, if Lyka was here there were probably other swipers too. In fact, he knew he had to get out. It was too dangerous. But before he could think how to do this he noticed another smell. A delirious, wonderful, soul-tickling scent like none he'd ever known. As soon as he smelled it he felt hypnotized, and could do nothing but follow where it led. Which was past the bathroom, over rugs and fish bones and cat fur, to the last room on the left.

He entered. Saw a room full of identical plants in pots. He recognized the plant from when he used to help his dad with the garden. It was catnip. Known to send cats into a state of delirium. He could do nothing but walk forward into the room to get closer to the plants.

Just as the wonderful scent had taken over every

part of his brain, Barney heard a faint and high-pitched voice behind him.

'Meee-*ow*,' it said.

It was obviously an order to attack as the next thing Barney knew, something was covering him. Something soft, but pressing down hard on his back. Whatever it was blocked the smell of catnip and was bringing him to his senses again.

'Get off me,' he cried. 'Please, let me go.'

But he was now being pushed – or dragged – in what he realized was a cat blanket. 'Please, get off me!'

It was no good.

He was still being dragged out of the room, across the landing, his claws struggling to cling to the small woollen loops. But whoever was dragging him must have been strong because he kept being pulled with the same steady force. 'Look, this is a mistake. If you let me go I'll just leave. Honestly. No questions asked. Please, it's all a mistake. Let me go.'

Still no good.

His attacker seemed to be turning him round another corner into a different room. Pressing his face against the blanket he could see through it, but even with cat's eyes it was only shapes and shadows that didn't make much sense.

Then, eventually, he stopped moving and the pressure of the blanket lightened.

'All right, kittens,' came a voice he recognized. 'Release him.'

Kittens?

He had been *assaulted* by kittens?

It was true. The blanket peeled back and Barney was in a room full of bright light. He looked behind him, blinking, to see seven small kittens with giant ears, each biting the edge of the blanket. All seven of them like miniature Lykas. Through Barney's human eyes they would have looked cute, but now they looked like nasty little bullies. Barney turned, just in time to see Lyka and a couple of other swipers closing the door. Then she turned to her kittens. 'Well done, my babies.'

Barney looked back towards the voice he had heard, and saw Pumpkin sitting on top of an old, switched-off TV that must have once belonged to the real Polly Whipmire. Beside the TV was one of her old books. The book was called *How To Be A Thoroughly Nice Person To Pretty Much Everyone* by Tiffany Thoroughgood. And next to that were bones. And this time they didn't belong to a fish. They were more solid. Cat-sized, but missing a head.

Then Pumpkin spoke. 'Right, swipers, let him

have it.' And a large cat came up to Barney. He was a large, old tortoiseshell with a bit of a limp. There were other bits of him that looked like they were wounded – patches where his fur seemed thinner or not there at all. It gave him the look of someone who had been roughly put together like a rag doll. But he could certainly swipe, and fast and hard too. Barney hardly knew where he was as the cat's paws and claws sliced at him.

Then other swipers joined in. Lyka, the kittens, Pumpkin, the bronze and black tabby, all of them. And Barney was just a blur of pain and fear.

But then the door opened. The cats stopped and waited, as Barney looked desperately around for an escape. The door to the room was open but it was well-guarded on every side. And there she was, Miss Whipmire, with Maurice standing there behind her in the body he'd stolen from Barney.

'Well, well, well,' said Miss Whipmire. 'It looks like you swipers have managed to do something right for once.'

'Mum, what are you going to do to him?' asked Maurice, looking worried.

Miss Whipmire turned to her son. She would have liked to kill Barney there and then but doubted her child had the stomach for the wails. So she picked up Barney, who was dazed and throbbing with pain.

'Nothing, darling. Now, don't you worry about it. I'm going to take him for a little drive. You go and enjoy some catnip.'

'But Mum—'

'No more *buts*, darling,' snapped Miss Whipmire. 'We've talked about this.'

As Miss Whipmire started carrying him downstairs, Barney heard Pumpkin.

'Before you be goin', what about our sardines? Will you open some tins for us?'

Miss Whipmire turned, furious. 'No, you are getting too slow and fat. I think I need to keep you swipers a little bit hungrier.'

And the swipers stood out on the landing, mumbling their unhappiness as Miss Whipmire crunched her way over fish bones and out of the house, squeezing Barney breathlessly close.

'So, you thought you could come here and speak to my Maurice without me, did you? You really are a sly thing, aren't you? Oh, well, it looks like that's another subject you're bad at, doesn't it? Staying alive.'

And Barney left the foul, filthy hallway and was carried out into the cold, uncaring wind.

'Now, Mr No-hoper, let's grade your chance of survival,' Miss Whipmire hissed evilly, seconds before hurling him hard into the boot of her small yellow car. 'Let's give you an F. For Fatally Failing Feline.'

Then the blackness came, with the sound of the boot closing, along with all possible hope.

Miss Whipmire's Idea of Fun

The car sped along. There was only darkness and noise. The engine, the wind outside, full of warnings even a cat's ears can't understand. It was then that Barney began to feel truly desperate. The combination of panic, cat lungs, what felt like a thousand scratches and being trapped in the boot of a car was making it very difficult to breathe, and it was also very hard to stay standing upright. By the time the car stopped he must have lost his balance a hundred times. At least.

And once the car did stop there was a confusing and ominous silence. The boot didn't open. Nothing happened, and kept on not happening. It felt like hours.

Then, at long last, footsteps outside.

The boot opened.

It was dark, but felt almost like daylight compared to the impenetrable blackness of the boot.

Wind blew wildly all around, louder than Barney had ever heard, creating a temporary wild mane out of Miss Whipmire's hair.

Then a noise which filled Barney with horror. Water.

Miss Whipmire pulled him out of the car. But by now he was realizing what was about to happen.

'Why are you doing this?' he asked as Miss Whipmire began to walk.

'For fun, mainly. But there's also a practical reason. You see, Barney, if you stay alive and somehow manage to turn into a human again, you might say things which could get me into trouble.'

'I wouldn't. I promise.'

'It doesn't even matter if you mean that. You see, I can now tell you the real reason.'

Barney remembered what the Doberman had told him, and the name Miss Whipmire had mentioned as she carried him from the house. 'Maurice?'

Miss Whipmire nodded, unsurprised. 'I want to make sure my son stays human too.'

Barney realized something. 'So, if I die, he's human for ever?'

'Well, I just like to make doubly sure. After all, my son and I are human now. We have a long life ahead of us and I want to protect that life. He was the only one of my litter who survived. He was my miracle . . .' Barney was surprised to hear real love in her voice.

'Though, of course, we were forced to separate a long, long time ago. Anyway, I am a mother. And a good one, and I want what is best for my little kitten. And in this day and age that means being human. Or being *you*. So, once you're dead, I will know the back door is closed. The back door meaning you. And closed meaning dead. So my little darling will stay human for the rest of his life – and we can always be together.'

Barney stared beyond Miss Whipmire, past the river bank. There were buildings in the distance, and even though they didn't have their lights on he could see them. It was a clear night with a bright moon and stars, enabling him to make out sheds and warehouses.

He knew where they were.

They were on the outskirts of town. By the river. Two miles from home.

She held him tight inside her furry jacket, and kept walking with slow, careful steps until they reached the bridge. It was a bridge Barney knew well. In fact it was the location of his very first memory: playing Pooh Sticks with his mum and dad.

Miss Whipmire let out a kind of cold laugh.

The sound scraped Barney's nerves like a blunt knife.

Then Barney was taken out of her coat, which was patched with cat-skin that had once been her own, and held out at arm's length over the side of the bridge.

She stared at him for a moment, the way you stare at an expensive meal before you eat it, her eyes wide with a mad glee.

Her phone rang. She answered. Barney heard a muffled voice. His own.

'Mum . . .' said Maurice. 'Mum, don't.'

'I'm doing this for you, darling.'

'He wasn't the one who blew off your tail.'

'No, I know that . . .' Miss Whipmire's voice contained a grain of sadness now. Though only a grain. 'But we are going to get our revenge on the Freemans when we get to Thailand, don't worry. Right now we need to know there is no one who can separate us again, darling. If he stays alive we will always be worried.

'Maurice, hang on . . .' Miss Whipmire didn't switch the phone off but placed it in her pocket for a moment. 'Now, I really did want another pen pot, but I think this method's going to be a bit quicker and cleaner . . . You'll just be another drowned cat in a river.'

Barney heard the water, relentless, below.

'Goodbye, Barney Willow,' said Miss Whipmire.

And then she let go.

She looked over the edge. It was a shame she couldn't let Maurice join her. Still, it was a sight she could enjoy by herself. A cat, turning into a little black dot, and then a little white splash.

And then nothing at all.

'Now,' said Miss Whipmire, picking up the phone again. 'It's over. Do not worry about how it happened. All we've got to do is stick with the plan. You leave the house and go back to Mrs Willow, act as normal as you can so she doesn't get twitchy. Then I'll go home and sort everything out. And in the morning I'll wait for you on the street, and you'll have to lose that Rissa girl. Just tell her at the bus stop that you've left something at home. Then we can get a clear head start. A full day without suspicion. We'll be on the other side of the world before anyone knows . . .'

The Water

Barney fell fast through the air, staring at the stars, distant diamonds resting on a black satin sky, the last beautiful thing he thought he'd ever see. Then his body twisted and righted itself so his paws were facing the water.

Down and down and—

Splash.

He hit the water hard with his paws. He'd fallen so fast it felt harder than water. And then he was in it, in the freezing, dirty, mammoth river, being pulled along by the current.

'Help!' he miaowed, trying to keep his head up. 'Somebody!'

But it was no good.

He glanced at the river bank.

The large empty buildings were sliding by at the speed of the water. He looked to the other bank, on his right side. It was even further, and not a house or building or person in sight. Just a jagged fringe of wild grass, too far away to offer any hope.

Barney kicked desperately with all his legs, and it took every single piece of energy simply to keep his head out of the water.

'Swim,' he told himself. 'Come on . . . *swim.*'

He tried to head towards the left bank because it was slightly closer. But the current was getting faster. It was like being a piece of dust shooting up a vacuum cleaner. He had never felt so small and useless and weak.

Then he realized why the water was speeding up. He was heading towards the weir. Even if he managed to keep his head above the river for another ten minutes it would be no good – he'd reach the weir and drown for sure.

Think . . . think . . . think . . .

But the voice in his head quickly changed.

Sink . . . sink . . . sink . . .

He was going to die, under a thousand shining stars.

Stars!

He knew Rissa's barge was two-minutes' walk from the weir, moored on the left bank. In fact, he realized he could just about see it ahead, its strip of low windows softly lighting the water.

And he was sure he could see Rissa out on deck, staring up at the stars with her telescope.

But the barge was still miles away. Cat miles, anyway. And although the current might have been carrying him in the right direction, he was being sent in a straight line, not a diagonal one. So he tried to angle himself, using every last grain of strength to paddle his tired, cold, stiff legs towards the barge.

Slowly he made some progress, but slowly wasn't good enough. There was no way he would be able to reach the barge. He'd seen enough triangles in maths lessons to know the angle wasn't sharp enough.

And even if it was, it would be impossible to climb on board.

Yet he kept going. He remembered being in a swimming pool wearing his pyjamas for a life-saving badge, and having to give up because his legs were too tired. His freezing legs were ten times as tired now, but being a cat had somehow helped him find a courage and determination he never knew were there.

He thought of nothing but the barge, and the Fairweathers' warm home inside as he tried to block out how cold and heavy the water was starting to feel.

Help! he miaowed when he could swim no more. *Rissa! Help! Help!*

Her silhouette stayed watching the star-strewn sky.

His head slipped under water, then back up into air again.

Rissa! Someone! Anyone!

She moved.

He was sure she moved.

She stood up, looked out at the water.

'*Rissa!*'

To his horror she sat down again. But then she lowered the telescope and looked out across the water.

As she did so Barney kicked all four of his legs in frantic desperation to keep his head as high and visible as possible.

His friend left the telescope and went inside the barge. At first he thought she hadn't seen him. But a moment later she came back out again with a man with a beard. Her dad. In a moment that seemed like for ever, he too had a look through the telescope.

Barney called out.

He didn't even bother with words this time. Words which wouldn't be understood.

He just made the loudest wailing miaow he could manage. A miaow that exhausted him. A miaow fuelled by every miserable moment since his parents' divorce.

They heard it. Saw him. Rissa's dad stood up and, without thinking, jumped into the water and started swimming.

Hold on, Barney told himself. *Just one more minute.*

Just hold on . . .

Hold on . . .

Hold . . .

The Barge

. . . On.

It was just enough.

He held on.

Rissa's dad reached him, his hand grabbing Barney's belly at the moment he was about to be pulled under.

'You're OK, little fellow,' Mr Fairweather said, himself exhausted, but determined to keep the cat above water as he made a shattering one-arm swim back to the barge.

Once there he quickly got Barney inside. Then Rissa and her mother attended to him in their long, warm and very thin living room while Mr Fairweather had a bath.

Barney had met Rissa's parents before, and liked them, but to be perfectly honest he had found them a little bit odd.

They lived on a barge, for a start. And they didn't even *own* a TV, let alone watch one. And they could spend hours talking about star formations. They had a computer but he'd never seen it. They did have a phone too, but one that looked like it came from 1973. And Rissa's dad had his big beard and wore long woolly jumpers with holes in them almost down to his knees, and made vegetarian meals full of strange ingredients like quinoa and buckwheat.

He was a carpenter, and Rissa's mum an artist. She painted pictures of plants and had them all over the walls. She had really long hair and naturally rosy cheeks and wore dungarees. She seemed to be in a state of extreme happiness all the time.

Their names were Robert and Sarah, which were the only ordinary things about them.

But Barney was now totally convinced they were the very best people you could hope to meet.

While Rissa dried Barney with a warm towel, her mum fed him pieces of the most delicious cheese he'd ever tasted in his life.

'This is Cornish Yarg,' she told him in a voice as warm as the stove which heated the room. 'The best cheese in the world. But I'm from Cornwall so I'm biased.'

She gave him another large yellow crumb.

'You poor little thing,' she was saying. 'You're so hungry.'

Rissa stroked behind his ear. 'It's that cat, you know, the one I told you about . . . The one that Miss Whipmire locked up. The one all those other cats were chasing after.'

Her mum looked puzzled. She loved her daughter, but what she'd told her and Robert that evening was rather a lot to take in. 'Oh, that's weird. Are you sure it's the same cat?'

'Yep. Same white patch. Same eyes.'

Rissa studied him.

Rissa, Barney miaowed.

'There's something strange about you,' his friend said, tenderly stroking his ear in a way that made him feel embarrassed. 'I really feel like I've known you for ages.'

You have! You have!

She stared at him a bit more, and then shook her head as if shaking away a silly and impossible thought.

'What do you think happened to him?' Rissa asked. 'Do you think those cats chased him into the water? Or do you think it had something to do with Miss Whipmire?'

'Well, don't worry. We've told the animal helpline. I'm sure they'll look into Miss Whipmire.'

Rissa thought about mentioning the trip to the cattery but didn't. She knew her parents would say she should tell Barney's mum, but Mrs Willow had enough on her plate right now.

She sighed bleakly. 'What with the cats, and with Barney being so odd this morning and running away before school, it's really been a weird day, Mum.'

I didn't run away. That wasn't me.

Barney saw that Rissa was looking sad, and he tried to comfort her by rubbing his head into her hand.

'You really like Barney, don't you?' said her mum, her eyes twinkling like the stars outside the porthole.

'Yes, I suppose I do.' Rissa's words caused Barney to feel embarrassed, and he was thankful for the furry face, which concealed his blush.

Rissa's voice changed. 'But Barns . . . I mean, Barney can be so annoying sometimes. Like today! Acting so weird this morning, and me thinking he'd run away for ever or something, and then just turning up at the end of the day . . . And not even bothering to phone here when he got home, after I hadn't been in school all afternoon. Then having to find out from his mum! What was that all about?'

'I don't know, darling,' her mum said as water lapped gently against the barge. 'I'm sure there's an explanation. He's a good boy, I know it.'

Barney knew that all the bits of information were there in Rissa's brain, like Lego. If only she could click them all together and make the truth.

Carrot Cake

After the cheese, the Fairweathers gave Barney some home-made carrot cake, cut up really small and placed in a bowl.

Then they sat him down on a warm rug. 'Oh, look,' said Rissa's mum sadly. 'He's got scratches all over him.'

'Mum,' said Rissa. 'Can he stay with us?'

'Of course he can. If he wants to. Can't he, Robert?'

Rissa's dad looked over at Barney from an old wooden chair as he played a soft melody on his guitar. 'You'd be very welcome, so long as you realize that's not a swimming pool out there.'

Rissa's mum poured some milk, which Barney lapped up as quickly as he could. It was delicious, and full of thousands of tastes and aromas he'd never known before.

Rissa sat down next to him on the rug, and stroked him. 'You're quite lucky to be a cat,' she told him.

'Because it means you don't have to pay too much attention to human beings.'

'That's not very cheerful, Rissa,' said her dad.

'Well, I know.' She sighed, and her hand came to a standstill on her friend's fur. 'It's just Barney.'

Her mum opened her sketchbook, started drawing her daughter and the cat with a piece of charcoal. 'I'm sure there's an explanation,' she repeated.

'I hope the old Barney's back tomorrow so I can have a best friend again.'

'Thought you wanted him to be more than that?'

This time Rissa blushed along with Barney.

'Changed my mind. No boyfriends till I'm at least eighteen! And it won't be Barney Willow! Anyway, best friends are more important than boyfriends.'

'One day you'll realize they can be both,' her mum said.

Barney looked up at Rissa's face. She seemed unhappy. And it hurt him to know that he was the cause.

I'm still here.

She stroked his chin. 'Poor cat. You're safe now.'

And then her dad started singing a made-up song. He called it 'A Cat Shanty'.

'Oh, you're safe now, cat, so don't you worry,
Oh, you're dry and warm and there's no hurry.
Oh, you might as well stay right here,
For a day, a week, or even a year . . . '

It was tempting. To stay here, with his best friend and her lovely parents, being fed cheese and carrot cake in the warmth of this barge.

And he certainly was sleepy.

Really sleepy.

249

Yes. Why not? Why not stay here?

As he stared up at the Fairweathers' loving, smiling faces he felt himself dissolving into darkness and a deep, deep sleep, in which he saw nothing but a shining green eye, glistening with answers.

I am Barney

Barney woke.

It was still night outside the windows of the barge, and the stars remained in the sky. He was alone on the rug, exactly as Rissa and her parents had left him.

He could hear the river lapping at the barge. He looked up at the wooden walls and the paintings of plants. One was of a cactus in a desert, with its long shadow stretching back across the sand. It looked more beautiful than any painting he had ever seen.

He could see Robert's guitar lying in the corner of the room next to the tiny kitchen area, and the remainder of the marmalade-flavoured carrot cake lying in a saucer near his front paws.

There are worse lives, he thought to himself, *than the life of a cat on a barge. Being warm, sleeping on a soft rug.*

He could stay here.

Safe.

For ever.

But then he remembered. His dad was alive. And

right now his mum was living with a former cat. And what if that former cat was as deadly as that former cat's mother? If that was the case his mum and Rissa could be in danger. *No.* He had to solve this. Somehow, he had to become human again. All he needed was to find out how, and he had a feeling he knew who'd be able to tell him. He didn't know why, but he kept on thinking of the Terrorcat and that strange, sad green eye staring at him, and the warmth he had felt inside. The feeling that he had something to say but hadn't.

Barney looked at the time on the old wooden clock on the wall.

It was half-past five in the morning.

Before he left he had some more milk, which had been left out for him, along with a nibble of the carrot cake too, as he knew he'd need all the strength he could get.

Then he had an idea.

Slowly, with his paws, he picked apart at the cake until it was a thousand little crumbs. Then he carefully pawed the crumbs onto the floor and shaped them into words on the light wooden floorboards:

I am Barney

It took him ages. Then he left, out of a tiny open window in the bathroom, and landed easily on the grass of the river bank.

He headed off in the direction of town, thinking about the shining green eye of the Terrorcat he had seen in his dream.

Rissa Realizes

Rissa woke before her parents. She stepped out of her little cabin in her normal morning haze and looked for the cat.

'Here, kitty-cat, where are you?'

And then she saw the crumbs on the floor. At first that is all they were. Just crumbs. But then she saw the crumbs had fallen into the shape of words, and she read the words and gasped as something the cattery owner – whoever he really was – had said yesterday afternoon came back into her head.

He might have come to you but you didn't recognize him. Trust me, keep your mind open to the impossible and you will find the truth.

Rissa's heart drum-rolled. And she quickly got ready and put on her coat to go and look for her friend.

The Terrorcat (and the Stillness of Things)

Barney reached the right house, opposite the park, but there was no sign of the one-eyed cat that always sat there every morning when he walked Guster. There was nothing in the window except an empty vase. Barney sat on the pavement a while, feeling vulnerable.

But there were no cats around.

Maybe they were too scared to come anywhere near the Terrorcat. Yes, that was probably it. In which case, maybe *he* should have been too scared to go anywhere near the Terrorcat. Still, he waited.

As he did, he observed his surroundings. The park. With the same trees and bushes and flower beds that had been there two days ago when he'd been human.

He had a weird feeling.

Like the world told the same lie over and over. The lie that things didn't change. That things stayed as still as the empty morning air.

And it was easy to keep the lie going because

most of the time things really *didn't* change.

Each Monday was like the last, give or take a few details. You saw the same faces every day, ate similar food week by week, did a lot of the same stuff. But the stillness of things made it worse when changes happened. Like when a shark pops out of an ocean to gobble a fisherman. Or like when his dad and his mum told him, 'We're not going to live together any more.' Or when, one day, his dad wasn't there to tell him anything at all.

An old woman was hobbling up the road with a pint of milk.

Barney had seen her quite a few times before. She lived somewhere on this road. She had hearing aids in both ears and was always fiddling with them with whichever hand wasn't holding the walking stick. Today she had both hands occupied so wasn't fiddling with anything, but Barney could tell she wanted to.

It took her a century to walk up the street. When she got to where Barney was, the old lady's eyes looked down with the same kindness she had always shown him as a human.

'Hello, sweetheart.'

Hello.

And then he realized.

She was going into number 22, and number 22 was the Terrorcat's house. And she was going so slowly Barney would easily be able to sneak inside, even if she hadn't turned to him and said, 'Come on, sweetheart. You look like you could do with some milk. Come on. Come inside.'

Inside: mouldy wallpaper, ancient carpet, black and white framed photos, unopened envelopes, and the deafening sound of breakfast TV presenters filling every corner.

But no cat.

Not in the hallway or the living room.

Then . . .

A voice from above:

'Hello.'

There he was at the top of the stairs, half in shadow, his one eye shining down like a solitary star on a cloudy night.

Barney realized he was expected to say something.

'Hello . . . Mr Terrorcat,' he said nervously. 'I'm Barney Willow. I'm not actually a cat. I just came to see you because yesterday you saved me from Pumpkin and those other swipers, and I thought you would . . . I thought you would know how I could turn back into a human. I thought as you obviously have powers . . .

I wondered . . . maybe you could do it for me?'

The Terrorcat sat in the same ominous silence so Barney stepped closer to the stairs. 'I really want to be a human. I want to be me again.'

Barney saw the old lady in the kitchen and her crooked hand beckoning him towards a saucer of milk. 'Come on, sweetheart.'

It was then the Terrorcat decided to speak, staying in exactly the same spot. His voice seemed to have a forced calm, but Barney's ears detected a troubled wavering.

'What made you change your mind?'

Barney had no clue as to what this meant. 'Sorry? I don't understand.'

The Terrorcat studied Barney.

'You wanted to be someone else. Anyone else. Even a cat. Or you wouldn't have been able to change.'

Barney closed his eyes, and in his memory saw torn pieces of paper flying in the wind, and remembered exactly how he had felt on Wednesday evening.

'I was stupid. I'd
had a bad day.' Barney
reconsidered. 'I'd had
a bad two years.'

'Two years?'

'My mum and dad
got divorced then, and
it's like everything
since has been cursed.
Everything. I went to
a terrible new school
with this demon head

teacher, who I now know is actually a cat, and with this
evil kid called Gavin who is just a nightmare. Then, on
top of all that, my dad disappeared.'

'*Pickles!*' It was the old lady, shouting even louder
than the people on TV.

'That's what she calls me,' said the Terrorcat softly.
'Not good for the cred, but I live with it.'

'Come on, you two kitty-cats, get some milk.'

The Terrorcat didn't move. Just stayed there, King
of the Stairs.

'You were saying? About your dad.'

'He wasn't living with us. He was living on his
own in a little flat. But one day he ran away. I don't

259

know why. No one knows. No one knows anything except that he was selfish, because he didn't leave a note or anything and never came to explain.'

They were called again for some milk, and then the old lady gave up and hobbled back to the living room and her TV.

'You are wrong,' said the Terrorcat.

Barney was surprised. 'What?'

'He came to see you, but he was thrown back out on the street. There was no way he could explain what he was going through. But he never stopped loving you.'

'I don't understand.'

The Terrorcat came downstairs, tackling each stair carefully. It seemed strange. A cat with superpowers worrying about how to handle a staircase.

When he was right up close, Barney stared into the speckled green of the cat's one eye and felt scared, as though he'd walked into a trap.

'More to me than meets the eye.' The Terrorcat then gestured with his head towards the kitchen. 'Come. Let's have some milk.'

Barney followed reluctantly.

They drank from the same bowl, and Barney would have loved the soothing creamy liquid on his dry tongue if it hadn't been for the fear prickling his whiskers.

'How do you know about my dad . . .' Then Barney had a thought. 'Are you psychic? Can you read minds?'

The Terrorcat spluttered on his milk. 'It's all a lie,' he said. 'This whole Terrorcat thing. I've no magic powers. The cats find it easy to believe because of how I look – with the eye. But really that just proves my lack of power. You see – like you, I wasn't always a cat. I was a human, too. And on my very first day as a cat I got into a fight with a Siamese.'

Barney thought of Miss Whipmire. 'Siamese?'

'Yes. I told her my name and everything, and she hated humans, and had a mean set of paws. That's how I lost the eye . . . Never seen her since, though.'

That certainly *did* sound like Miss Whipmire.

'The old lady took me in. Looked after me. Got me stitched up at the vet's . . .'

'So why "the Terrorcat"?'

'Well, survival. That thing about cats having nine lives is not true. I realized the way to stop fear was to become fear itself. I had no powers, not like real cats. But I looked scary. Plus . . .'

The Terrorcat hesitated, took a slow lap of the milk and seemed to be mulling something over. 'Plus,

I was good at selling when I was human, at putting on an act,' he said at long last. 'That was my only talent. That's the only real talent I've ever had. So when I was mistaken by a ginger moggy for the legendary Terrorcat, I said, "That's me." It was easy.'

Wasn't always a cat . . .

On my first day . . .

Good at selling . . .

'So . . . if you're not psychic, how do you know so much about my dad?'

Barney gaped into the eye. Up close, he knew that was what brought him here, like a moth to a lightbulb. Not the eye itself but the soul shining inside. He knew that soul better than he knew anything in the world.

The Terrorcat said nothing for a moment as a drop of milk slipped off his chin into the bowl. There wasn't an actual smile, but Barney sensed one. 'You already know.'

It was true. Barney knew. How could he not, this close to the human he loved as much as any other, even if that human was now a cat?

'Yes, Dad. I do.'

A Heavy Truth

It took a moment for it to sink in.

Several moments, actually. And long ones.

He wanted to hug his dad, and his dad wanted to hug him back, but hugging's not so easy when you're a cat, so they purred mutual love and head-nuzzled, which was as close as they could get.

But Barney began to feel angry. And the anger brought questions.

Why did it happen?
ANSWER: His dad had been feeling sad, and had seen a happy cat basking in the sun.

But why had he wanted to be a cat in the first place, when he had a son who loved him?
ANSWER (a rubbish one, in Barney's opinion): Because since the divorce he didn't see that much of him. And because he was just feeling sorry for himself.

Did he think of Barney?
ANSWER: Every moment of every day, which is why he waited at the window each morning to see him on the way to the park with Guster (who always stopped him getting any closer). He said he thought of everything. Of the apple and blackberry crumble he used to enjoy. Of the long walks in Bluebell Wood that he didn't dare visit now, owing to all the dogs that went there. He thought of his dream of opening a garden centre. And of swimming backstroke in a pool.

So what happened to the cat that turned into him?

ANSWER: He's working at a cattery in Edgarton. He was a kind creature and had wanted to help other cats who had to stay in the most rotten cattery in the world. So now Edgarton Cattery is a nice place, and one where cats who have been there wish their owners would go on holiday for ever.

Did he know how they could turn back into humans?

ANSWER: Yes. Find the cats who'd turned into them, and wish they were human again.

Barney mulled this over.

'So, why didn't you go to Edgarton and change back?'

Barney's dad looked cautious, the way cats do when they stand looking at snow, not knowing where to step. 'He came and found *me*. A month ago. He was feeling guilty. And he said he wanted to be a cat again and all I had to do was wish I was a human . . .'

'So what happened?' asked Barney.

His dad sighed. 'Nothing. I stayed like this.'

'But, why? Does it take longer? Might it still happen?'

'No. It's supposed to be quicker, instantaneous, when you wish back, because it's a shorter distance to your own self than it is to someone else's. That's the theory.'

'So why are you still a cat?'

Barney's dad dipped his head. 'I . . . I . . . didn't want to be *me* enough.'

This made Barney so furious he felt his claws protrude. 'Dad! Don't you realize how worried everyone's been about you?! I've had nightmares and everything . . .'

Barney's dad looked sad. His eye couldn't cry but Barney felt the invisible tears.

'Yes, I'm sorry. But that wasn't enough.'

'*What?*' hissed Barney.

The old lady came into the kitchen to put the kettle on. 'Now, now, sweethearts . . . behave yourselves. We are all friends here, aren't we, Pickles?'

'Look,' continued the cat who had once been known as Neil Willow. 'I wanted more than anything for you and your mum to know I was safe, and if I could have pressed a button for you to stop worrying I'd have pressed it. But the more I hated myself for upsetting you and your mum, the less happy I was with myself. The human me. Turns out you have to actually like yourself to become yourself . . .'

'I don't understand.'

'I wasn't the best father,' his dad went on. 'And I certainly wasn't a good employee at Blandford Garden Centre any more. And so, as a human, I was too weak. I'd become a miserable grump, to be honest, son. And so I couldn't be happy with who I was and switch back once I'd changed.'

'So you were trapped?'

His dad hesitated.

The old woman made her cup of tea then hobbled away. 'Be good, kitties,' she croaked.

'Well, I suppose so,' Barney's dad said uncertainly in answer to his son's question.

'But . . . ?' said Barney, sensing there was more.

'But I don't want you to pity me. The thing is, in a way there is a good side to being a cat. You know, I am respected. I have a warm home. I am fed. I have milk to drink . . .'

Barney was disappointed. 'But don't you want to live with us? As a human?'

Mr Willow gently rested his head against his son's and kept it there. 'Barney, I don't think your mum would want that. And she's right. We made each other unhappy, and that made you unhappy.'

The truth of these words weighed Barney down. He was right. His mum and dad were separated, whatever species they were. 'OK, Dad. Well, at least you're alive.'

Barney had a million more things to say, but right now he said none of them, choosing to listen to the simple love he felt from his father's purr.

Hiding in the Bush

They had a bit more milk and went into the living room.

There were adverts on TV. Fluffy Labrador puppies advertising toilet paper. It was like watching a horror movie. Then the sound of barking, outside.

Out of the window, a boy went past walking his dog. The dog was straining desperately on his lead.

'Did you see that?' Barney asked his father. 'It's him. I mean, *me*. Walking Guster . . .' He looked back to the door. 'How do you get out of here?'

His dad's eye shone with concern. 'Barney, it's dangerous out there. Guster isn't our friend any more. He hates us. He wants to kill us. And what about your other self? The you-who-isn't-you. He could be any cat. The one who turned into me had honourable reasons, but there's no knowing what your cat's reasons were.'

'He wants to live with his mum,' said Barney. 'But his mum's evil. In fact . . .'

269

Barney stared at the white stitching on his dad's eye socket and was about to tell him that Miss Whipmire was probably responsible for that too, but realized there wasn't time right now.

'Doesn't sound good.'

'No. It's not. Which is why I've got to speak to Guster.'

Barney's dad was on the verge of responding when his son walked out of the room towards the front door. He followed, caught up with him in the hallway. 'No. The cat flap's this way.'

And they headed out together, down an alley, across the road and up the little tarmac slope into the park.

They hid in a bush.

Watching.

'Stay as quiet as you can,' Barney's dad purr-whispered (or rather, to use the proper expression, whis*purred*). 'Guster's heading over.'

It was true. Within seconds, there was Guster's wet nose poking through the leaves.

'Good gracious,' Guster was saying to himself. 'One does believe one can smell something of the feline persuasion lurking in the area. Come on, you vile thwarted tinch-tigers, where are you?'

'We're here,' announced Barney.

Barney's dad couldn't believe it. 'What are you *doing*?'

But Barney carried on. 'Guster, it's *me*. Barney.'

'*You*,' growled Guster, spotting Barney behind the leaves. 'The trespasser!'

'No. I've never trespassed. Just listen. Please. That boy who's brought you to the park isn't me.'

Guster was furious. 'Right, that's my quota! One cannot take any more of such insolence. I am going to have to kill you and your acquaintance.'

His head reached right into the bush, baring teeth.

'*Run!*' said Barney's dad.

But Barney was stuck. Tangled amid twigs.

Mr Willow ran back, jumping in front of his son to save him.

Guster was right there now, straight ahead of Barney's dad, with every single deadly tooth on display. 'To defy me is to defy my long-dead king. Oh, well, you first then.'

'You can't,' said the cat formerly known as Neil Willow. 'I am the Terrorcat.'

'The Terror-*what*?'

'I have powers you could not dream of.'

But, unlike the cat population of Blandford, Guster had never heard of the Terrorcat and so didn't really care. 'Well, you didn't use them last time I saw you. When you tried to speak to me through the kitchen window.'

Barney desperately tried to free himself. 'Dad, I'm sorry – you were right. Just run or he'll kill both of us.'

'No way . . .' And then Mr Willow had an idea. 'Guster, listen, you can kill us in a second . . . Just hear me out.' He tried to think. 'You . . . *like the snow*.'

The spaniel's jaws froze in midair.

'In winter you run in it with your head low and your tongue out,' Barney's dad blurted. 'And . . . and we washed you once, in the bath, but only once, because you went crazy when the water went in your eyes . . . and . . . and . . . You always liked sticking your head out of the window . . . and . . .'

Barney could see this might be working, so helped his dad out. 'And you hate chocolate! Even nice human chocolate. When I gave you some you spat it on the carpet. But you love it when I scratch your tummy.'

Guster's jaws closed. 'One can't abide chocolate, that is true . . . *How do you know all this? Who supplied your information?*'

'Guster. It's me, Barney. And this is Dad. You have to believe us.'

Guster was looking very confused. But then he was suddenly yanked out of the bush, his lead clipped on. Barney-Who-Wasn't-Barney, or rather, Maurice, was pulling the spaniel hastily out of the park.

'We've got to follow them,' Barney said, finally freeing himself from the last twig. This time his dad reluctantly agreed.

They jogged behind in silence for a while, considering what to do next. Eventually Barney decided to speak to his body snatcher.

'Maurice,' he said. 'Maurice!'

And Barney watched his former body stop and turn round. He looked shocked, as if he thought he was seeing a ghost.

273

'Go away,' Maurice said.

'No. I won't. I can't. I don't want to be a cat any more.' And Barney wished as hard as he could wish, closing his eyes and urging himself to enter his old body again, but . . . nothing.

'Trust me, if you know what is good for you, you will run far, far from here.' It sounded more like a warning than a threat, as though Maurice actually wanted to help them.

Barney felt his dad nudge up against him when Maurice and Guster walked on. 'I think we should do as he says.'

Barney waited, watching as Maurice yanked an even more perplexed Guster forward round the next corner. Before he vanished out of view completely, Maurice went stiff with fear.

'Come on, Dad,' Barney said, looking at his father's nervous face. 'Let's see what's happening.'

When Barney reached the corner he quickly saw the reason for Maurice's fear. It was Gavin, walking to the bus stop with his mates Alfie Croker and Rodney Wirebrush.

'Oi, Barney,' Gavin shouted to Maurice. 'Oi, you weirdo! What happened to you yesterday?'

Maurice said nothing.

Gavin was up close now, so enjoying himself he hadn't noticed the cats. 'I'm speaking to you. Speak, you freak! Speak!'

Barney was terrified as Gavin pushed Maurice against the wall.

He thinks it's me, he thought. *That should be me against the wall.*

Guster just grumbled nervously. 'Crikey! Oh good grief! Oh my word!'

'We should leave,' Barney's dad was saying. 'This isn't our business.'

'No, Dad,' Barney said quickly. 'This is exactly our business.'

Then he noticed something. When he looked at the situation from cat level, he could see that he was roughly the same height as Gavin. Not as a cat, obviously, but as a human. OK, so Gavin *was* a little taller than Barney's true self but the difference wasn't really that much. Two inches. No more. He suddenly realized Gavin was only as scary as you *let* him be. Barney had no more reason to fear him than the feline population of Blandford had reason to fear the Terrorcat.

'The donkey,' Barney said to Maurice.

'What?' gargled Maurice, petrified, as Gavin's hand kept pressing up against his neck.

'Mention the donkey. You know, the cuddly one he sleeps with on his bed. It's called Eeyore.'

And Maurice remembered. The cuddly donkey from the room he'd had a thousand nightmares about.

'Donkey,' he said, his voice weak and blank at first. Gavin snarled. '*What?*'

Maurice steeled himself. 'I'll tell your friends about who you've had to share a bed with ever since your mum noticed you'd wet the—'

Gavin's eyes were filled with dread. 'How do you *know?*' he said. 'You've never been to my house.'

'If only.'

Meanwhile Rodney and Alfie had stopped laughing.

'What's he talking about?' asked Rodney.

'Yeah. What's Willow mean?' added Alfie.

'I'll tell them,' said Maurice. 'I promise you. Oh, and the damp sheets.'

'Yes,' growled Guster, not having a clue about what was going on. 'He most certainly will.'

Gavin went purple with rage, and experienced the kind of fear that only came to him in his nightmares. A few moments later Alfie was pointing to the pavement. A puddle was emerging around Gavin's feet.

'He's wetting himself! Look! Look!'

Alfie and Rodney were bent double, laughing even more.

'Shut up!' shouted Gavin. 'Shut up, skinny rake!' he said to Rodney Wirebrush. 'Shut up, dog breath!' he said to Alfie Croker. But even Gavin realized, as his friends kept laughing, that he'd suddenly just lost his bully powers. He walked away, fast, beckoning for his friends to follow, but they didn't – they walked off in the other direction, laughing a laughter that burned into Gavin as he began jogging towards home.

Barney saw his own freckled, but actually not-bad-looking, face stare back down at him. Maurice seemed thankful, but didn't say so. Instead he ran back to a house that wasn't rightly his, pulling the half-reluctant King Charles spaniel behind him.

A Small Circle of Believability (or, the Wish He Wished He'd Never Wished)

The sky was full of thick, grey, puffy clouds, as if the whole of Blandford was tucked under the same duvet.

But Barney wasn't feeling very snug as he waited with his dad outside the front door, which had been deliberately closed far too quickly for them to get inside.

He could hear his mum's voice behind it, talking to the boy she thought was her son. Barney couldn't hear the words, though, just the tone. Worried, maybe a little cross.

Two cats prowled by, made eye contact with Barney's dad, then ran down the street.

'See who that was?' said one in a panic.

'*The Terrorcat!*' confirmed the other with dread.

Barney turned to his dad. They both laughed, cat-style. But then Barney thought of something.

'I don't get it,' he said. 'I was there just then, with

Maurice, and I was wishing to be in my own body again, but it didn't happen. I'm still a cat.'

His dad nodded. 'You have to *really* want it.'

'I do.'

'No, *really*,' his dad explained. 'I mean, I want my old life back too, but it's not enough. You see, if there's a part of you that is still unhappy with who you were, then it won't happen. You have to want to be you more than Maurice does. More than you've ever wanted anything. You have to accept everything in your life, all the things you can't change. You have to truly want to be Barney Willow.'

Barney considered.

His old life:

School. Gavin. Miss Whipmire. Rugby. Nicknames. A mum in fast-forward. Long weeks and weekends of infinite nothingness.

It was hard to find the happiness. The reasons to be grateful.

Mr Willow decided it was time to tell his son something he knew he should have said a long time ago and hadn't been able to, not even in Barney's dreams. 'None of it was your fault, you know. The divorce, I mean. It was about me and your mum, that's all.'

As his dad said this he sniffed one of the pot plants

by the door, and the scent soothed him. 'At least there will always be plants.'

Barney sighed, feeling more fed up than ever that he was trapped in this body. In cat fancy-dress for possibly the rest of his life. 'I just wish I'd never wished.'

'Well, you did. And now you've just got to wish even harder,' said his dad.

His mum's voice, behind the door. Clearer this time: 'Barney, shouldn't you be going to school? You don't want to be late. You were in trouble enough yesterday.'

There was a response. But not one they could hear properly.

And then footsteps coming from the street.

Barney head-nudged his dad. 'That's Rissa.'

And it was.

Rissa, still ten-storeys high, but with new worry etched on her face. She looked down. Saw Barney by the doorstep. And this time – he was sure – she actually saw *Barney*.

'I read your message,' she said, confirming his hope. 'The one you made out of the crumbs. It's you, isn't it? You're Barney.'

Yes, said Barney, but, of course, reading a message made out of carrot cake didn't mean his friend could actually understand cat. But just in case, he added: *And this is my dad.*

Rissa crouched down to get as close to his level as she could. 'Can you nod your head?'

Barney nodded.

'And shake it?'

He did so.

She smiled, but her forehead said she was still worried. 'OK. Nod for yes, shake for no. Got it?'

Barney nodded.

'I'm going to tell your mum, OK?'

Barney shook his head. It wasn't OK.

'Why? Because of that other Barney?'

Barney nodded. So did his dad.

'Who is that other Barney . . . ? Is he a cat?'

Another nod.

'Is he dangerous?'

Cats can nod, but can't shrug their shoulders. She seemed to understand.

Rissa thought. 'But if he's even *possibly* dangerous we've got to tell your mum, haven't we?'

Nod.

'And she's not going to understand *you*, is she?'

Shake. She was right, Barney realized. There probably wasn't any other way.

So Rissa inhaled, hoping to find courage floating on the cool morning air, then stood up to ring the doorbell.

Barney's mum answered.

Oh, Elaine, I do miss you sometimes, said Barney's dad, unheard far below her.

'Mrs Willow,' said Rissa. 'Listen, I have something to tell you.' She picked up Barney. '*This* is your son.'

But Barney's mum couldn't believe this. She really physically couldn't. You see, the space in your brain for 'things you are prepared to believe in' gets smaller as you get older. Each year the area shrinks, like the age rings of a tree trunk in reverse, and Barney's mum was now forty-three years old, which left her with quite a small circle of believability.

'I'm sorry, Rissa,' she said, looking the wrong kind of concerned, 'but I really think you might need to see a doctor.'

Rissa stayed where she was. 'Please can I come inside? I think I can prove it.'

Barney's mum shook her head. 'Not with the cats, I'm afraid – Guster hates them. But you can come in on your own.'

Rissa kept holding Barney. 'OK, I'll do it here . . . Barney, are you a cat?'

Barney saw Rissa was looking at him, her eyebrows pleading for him to respond. Barney wasn't concentrating, though. His whiskers were curling, sensing a danger his brain couldn't translate.

'Go on, son,' said his dad, miaowing up from below. 'Nod your head.'

So Barney did. He nodded.

'There! Did you see—?'

Rissa stopped, because right behind Barney's mum she saw Barney. *Fake* Barney. Maurice – although, of course, Rissa didn't know that was his name.

'Hello, Rissa,' he said a little timidly.

'Don't pretend you know me,' she said, angrier than Barney had ever heard her. 'Anyway, *who* are you? And why are you doing this?' She almost spat the words.

Then Barney realized what his whiskers were trying to tell him:

A car.

A car slowing down.

A car slowing down and parking near the house, the low mumbling vibration of its engine sounding like an ominous purr.

Barney knew that sound, even though he wasn't a car person. Or a car cat.

He had heard it up close. Really close.

And the noise sent him right back to last night. In the dark, trapped. *It was Miss Whipmire's car.*

As Rissa and his mum continued to talk, Barney waited in his best friend's arms. He kept expecting his head teacher to appear. But she didn't.

'Dad,' he said. 'I think something's going on . . . '

And just at that moment Barney felt a massive jolt as the world spun sideways. Something had knocked Rissa, he realized, just as he saw his own back walking away from him.

'Hey!' shouted Rissa.

'*Maurice*,' Barney wailed. 'Where are you going?'

Then his mum stormed out onto the road. 'Barney! What on earth are you—?'

She stopped, noticing something. Someone.

'She's just seen Miss Whipmire,' Barney miaowed down to his dad.

'Miss Whipmire?'

'Yes. She's a former cat. A really evil *Siamese* cat.'

'Siamese . . . ?'

'Yes. And she wants to kill me. She's evil. I mean, deeply evil.'

Barney noticed his dad was getting further away from him, even though he was standing in the same spot.

No! Barney shouted, realizing Rissa was carrying him out onto the pavement. He shook his head about twenty times in three seconds but Rissa wasn't looking.

The next thing he knew, he could see her.

Miss Whipmire, Caramel herself, stepping out of her car while telling Maurice, 'Come to me, my darling boy.'

She spoke softly, tenderly, and then, when she turned to see Rissa and Barney, her face forced itself into a smile.

'Oh, hello, Risso.'

'It's Riss*a*, actually, miss.'

Miss Whipmire shrugged. 'A rose by another name would still prick your fingers. And, oh, you've found my cat. I've been looking for him everywhere.'

'This isn't your cat.'

'What's going on here?' This was Barney's mum, now out on the pavement. 'Oh, hello again, Miss Whipmire. What are you doing here?'

Miss Whipmire thought for a moment, survey-ing the street and its old semi-detached houses. A gaggle of schoolgirls in Blandford High uniforms had just appeared round the corner. A cat sat on a brick wall opposite. It was the ginger cat that hung round the school. The one that had chased Rissa and Barney.

Pumpkin.

Rissa recognized him too, because her hand suddenly tightened fearfully around Barney's middle.

'Mrs Willow,' said Miss Whipmire. 'I would really like to speak with you indoors.'

Barney's mum looked at who she thought was her son, standing strangely close to his head teacher. 'Barney? What's—?'

'Mum, just go inside. Miss Whipmire wants to talk with you.'

Mum, he's not your son!

'OK. I will. But I must say I'm finding this all very odd.'

Don't listen to him! He's a cat called Maurice!

'Mrs Willow,' said Rissa, 'don't do as they say. They might be dangerous.'

Yes! Listen to her!

Barney's mum gave Rissa another flustered look.

Miss Whipmire smiled. 'You just stay there, Rissa,' she said, fast as a mousetrap.

Rissa didn't know what was best. She looked down at Barney, who was shaking his head.

Follow, he miaowed. *Ignore her.*

And as he was carried forward he looked down at the doorstep, and all around, but there was nothing but an empty path and uninhabited flower beds. His dad was nowhere to be seen.

Human Things

Two things happened very quickly once they were inside the kitchen.

First thing:

Miss Whipmire dug her long unvarnished nails into Rissa's face while simultaneously yanking Barney from her grip.

Second thing:

Miss Whipmire waggled her thumb in the air as she warned Rissa and Barney's mum away.

'It's incredible,' she said, her voice making Barney think of bubbling cauldrons full of frogs. 'Humans have had opposable thumbs for over three million years, and yet hardly any of you know how to do the Fatal Thumb Death Press. The humans of Thailand invented it. Or Old Siam, I should say, home of my ancestors . . . One touch in the right part of the neck and we've a dead cat on our hands. Well, that would be true if this really *was* a cat.'

Barney stared at the fatal thumb. Then at Rissa and his mum, standing on the other side of the kitchen table.

Breakfast was still out.

He saw his mum's bowl of tasteless diet cardboard flakes (as he always called them), and then another bowl – full of milk but no cereal, with no spoon.

Only two days ago he'd been sitting at this table, eating out of that bowl, believing he had a pretty miserable existence. He'd been stupid.

Yes, school hadn't been much fun recently. But he had a warm home, full of nice human things, and a mum who loved him and the best best friend who'd ever lived. Life wasn't ever one ingredient. It was several. And some flavours were bad and some were good, but love was the strongest of all. If you were loved, you had everything. It was the milk that made the cereal of life worth tasting.

Meanwhile, as these near-death thoughts were bursting open in Barney's brain, Rissa was now staring worriedly over the table. 'Just let him go.'

Barney could see his mum thinking. Finally the truth had arrived, lighting her eyes. 'Oh, my goodness! Rissa, you were right, weren't you?'

'Afraid so.'

Miss Whipmire laughed. 'Yes. Everything you see, Mrs Willow, is an illusion. For instance, you see a human holding a cat. When in reality it is a cat holding a human.'

Barney saw his mum's eyes switch to anger, the way they sometimes used to when she had argued with his dad. Only Barney had never seen her look quite *this* cross.

'Put down my son, you evil . . .' Barney's mum was going to say 'woman', then 'cat', but eventually went for 'thing'.

'No,' Miss Whipmire refused. 'That's not going to happen. You see, everything is the opposite of normal from now on. So, the cat – that's me – and her son – that's my darling Maurice, who is waiting for me in the car – are going to stay together. Yes. We are going to run away and be happy after years of cruel separation.'

'But wait,' said Rissa. 'We weren't—'

'Now,' interrupted Miss Whipmire sharply. 'You humans can talk all you want but nothing will change a thing. Just like a cat's miaows never change a thing. So I suggest you listen, just for once, to what this cat has to say.'

Rissa wasn't to be silenced. 'But *we* didn't separate you two.'

Miss Whipmire viewed her coldly. 'No, Polly Whipmire did. The real one. But she's currently busy in her new office job.'

'What office job?' asked Rissa, stalling for time.

'Pen pot . . .' Miss Whipmire hissed. And just in case they didn't understand: 'She's dead.' Now she had even silenced Rissa. 'Anyhow, she didn't have children of her own so I needed to find one, grind him down, then get my son to follow him . . .'

As Barney listened he felt a weird prickling sensation on his skin.

'At first I told him he should try turning into Gavin

Needle,' Miss Whipmire continued, 'as that was the boy he lived with. But, although Gavin is quite an unhappy child, he never had the imagination to be anything other than what he is: a bully. And an idiot. So, in my new job, I went to the English teacher, Mr Waffler, and asked him to single out the boys in the school who had the best imaginations. In his sublime do-goody ignorance he gave me a list and I had a look. Barney was on that list, very near the top – even though he had only just joined the school, Mr Waffler had already singled him out as extremely imaginative.

I knew he was the boy who had once laughed when his dog ran after me, and I thought it would be a sweet punishment if I chose him as the human my darling Maurice would follow. But that wasn't the main reason. The main reason was that I had met his father in a dark alley one night shortly before I transformed. He was a cat. A silver cat. He told me he was really a human, I fought him out of disgust, took his eye. But, anyway, the name lodged in my mind somewhere. Neil *Willow*. And I knew that weak-minded fathers make weak-minded sons as apples don't fall far from trees. So I decided Barney was an easy target . . .'

Barney's mum was trembling and speechless. It

was too much for her to absorb. But Miss Whipmire's cruel words carried on. 'All I had to do was make him as miserable as possible and, being a head teacher, that was pretty easy. Then I sent Pumpkin to take a message to my son at the Needles' house and it was arranged. I knew, sooner or later, it would happen. And, when Barney was in my office staring at my cat calendar, I planted the idea in his brain. To be a cat, I told him, would really be the best thing he could imagine . . . And now my son and I are human, and no one will come and separate us.'

Barney's mum was shaking with fear and anger. 'But I'm a mother too. And that's *my* son. What do you need him for? You could just . . . leave him here. And go. We won't stop you.'

'A nice idea,' said Miss Whipmire, pretending it really was, 'but I'm going to take him just in case. Oh, and if you contact the police or go to the papers he'll be gone . . .'

Barney's mum was desperate as her son started to be carried away. 'Please! No!'

Miss Whipmire tutted. 'I wouldn't cry too much for him. After all, he obviously wasn't happy being your son. Or he wouldn't still be a cat.'

Miss Whipmire walked backwards, holding her thumb up like a weapon, as Barney saw his kitchen, his hallway, his mum, his best friend – his wonderful best friend – slipping away like a dream he didn't want to end.

The Wind in a Wish's Sails

Guster, upstairs in Barney's bedroom, was confused. The one-eyed cat kept telling him that he was, in fact, the man who used to live here. Neil Willow. Barney's dad.

But at least he wasn't barking any more. He was listening. And the more he listened, the more things started to make sense.

For instance, it had been most peculiar to see that black and white cat in Barney's bed. Even more peculiar, hours before that, to watch Barney climb in through the window of the downstairs toilet and stay there until morning. Why had he been, in the middle of the night, somewhere else? Unless he had been *someone* else. Someone who didn't live here in the first place.

'Guster, I'm telling you the truth.'

And Guster knew it, as sure as the eye that stared at him was green. 'Oh, the fool I've been. Such a blot upon my pride!'

Then they heard the commotion downstairs. Barney being carried into the hallway, his mum and Rissa begging Miss Whipmire to let him stay.

'We have to stop her!' said Guster. 'In the name of the king, we have to do something!'

So Guster charged hastily out of the room and down the stairs, just in time to catch Miss Whipmire opening the door.

He caught Barney's eye. 'I'm sorry, my liege.' Then he sank his teeth into Miss Whipmire's leg as hard as he could.

'Get off mee—owwww!'

But Guster wouldn't let go, not with Barney cheering him on from over Miss Whipmire's shoulder. And soon Rissa and Barney's mum were there too, grabbing her arm and straining to keep her thumb away from Barney's neck. Miss Whipmire called to Pumpkin on the other side of the pavement, who beckoned with his tail to Lyka further up the street, who beckoned with *her* tail to the other swipers hiding in doorways and behind bins.

'*Now!*'

Barney's dad ran out of the front door into the street, where fifty curtains were twitching all at the same time as the residents of Dullard Street wondered why so many cats had suddenly appeared as if from nowhere.

Barney's dad stood right in the middle of the road, and in the scariest cat voice he could manage he declared:

'I am the Terrorcat! If any of you feeble felines step one paw closer I will unleash terror! Big . . . terror! So stay where you are!'

The cats, about twenty of them, did as he said.

Not a paw forward, not a paw back.

Then Maurice got out of the car to help his mum.

'Here, Barney,' said Sheila, Mocha's owner, the nice but nosy lady who lived at number 33. 'What's going on?'

'I'm not Barney,' he said, and started running to help his mum.

Meanwhile, amid all this mayhem, as Guster kept biting, as Rissa and his mum kept pulling, the real Barney was closing his eyes.

I am not a cat.

I am Barney Willow.

And being Barney Willow is OK. More than OK. It's good.

Miss Whipmire is just a bitter, spiteful cat with a grudge . . .

Gavin Needle is just a stupid, frightened bully who cuddles donkeys . . .

Mum and Dad aren't together but that's not my fault . . .
I am lucky to have them.
I am lucky to have Rissa.
And, OK, I am not good at rugby.
I'm quite short and freckly and go to a horrible school, but I know the truth deep inside.
I am lucky to be me.
And I always was.
I just didn't realize it.

'Stay in the car!' Miss Whipmire's scream broke into Barney's thoughts. She was shouting at her son. 'I can handle this! Stay in the car! Don't get close to him! You're too weak! Don't let him make eye contact!'

Barney turned, saw the face that should be his, then gazed into his own human eyes.

'Maurice,' Barney said, 'if you change back, it will be OK. You won't have to return to the Needles. You could live with us. Guster would understand. I promise.'

'I would indeed!' confirmed Guster with a quick yap before chomping again on Miss Whipmire's leg.

Barney thought. 'Or if you really wanted to live with your mum, you could. No one would stop you.'

This in particular almost made Miss Whipmire combust with fury. 'Don't listen to them. You stay being a human. We'll be humans together. To be a cat is to be nothing! As a human you could live seven times as long, buy your own food in supermarkets, and never be separated from me! The humans have the best of this world ... not the cats! And humans are all vile and ungrateful things, so they've got no right to everything they have.'

Maurice thought. He'd never been the brightest of cats, but strong thoughts can shine lights in even the dimmest of brains sometimes.

And this was the thought Maurice was thinking:

Barney helped me when he was being bullied by Gavin, so not all humans can be all bad. And if Mum's lying about that, she might be lying about other things . . .

Plus, added to this thought was something else we should consider. Maurice was a good cat, as most cats are, and he didn't like any kind of bully. After all, he had lived with one before – did he want to live with another, even if that bully was, technically, his mum? But if his mum truly loved him, why did she want him to be something other than his true self? These questions worked like keys, opening up Maurice's mind, letting the wish that Barney was wishing shoot right in and make itself comfortable.

At the same time Miss Whipmire felt the increasing

weight on her left shoulder and knew what was happening. She called over to Pumpkin.

'I need help! Move. Help me! . . . That's Barney's father! There's no such thing as a Terrorcat, you idiotic swiper!'

'There is,' said Barney's dad. 'Oh, there very much is. Come one paw closer and you'll see.'

But it didn't matter if there was or there wasn't a Terrorcat. What mattered was what Pumpkin and the others had just heard.

'To be a cat is to be nothing?' Pumpkin hissed in disgust. 'That's a lie, that is. To be a cat is to be happy in your own fur. You was a no-good cat if you ever thought that! You can shove yer woofin' sardines in lemon-infused olive oil! I'm not working for such a low-life any more. I'm not a fireside. I've got principles! Come on, swipers, let's keep our dignity.'

And Pumpkin and Lyka and the rest of his gang strolled away, causing Miss Whipmire to become angrier than she'd ever been in her life. And the anger kept rising as she looked at her son out on the pavement, his face starting to get hairy.

His back beginning to hunch.

His ears sharpening.

His tail pushing through his shirt.

The anger gave Miss Whipmire strength. She freed her arm from the grip of Rissa and Barney's mum, who went flying onto the carpet. Then she kicked her leg, sending a winded Guster rolling back to the base of the stairs.

But all the time Barney was transforming too. He heard his dad encouraging him. 'She's wrong, son. The apple's fallen far from the tree. You're not me. Your mind's stronger than mine ever was . . . You can do it. You can do it, Barney.' And Barney could feel it, the change branching through his body. Even though right now he was still much closer to cat than human, and it was all too easy for Miss Whipmire to do what she did next. Namely, whack him down against the wooden chest in the hallway and press her thumb into his neck.

As she did so, Barney felt a pain beyond anything to which the name of pain is given. She pressed down in the right spot. Right on a nerve. He could hardly breathe. But he could still hear his head teacher's voice talking to her son.

'Well, Maurice, I'm going to stop this right now. In about five seconds, there'll be no Barney Willow. *You'll* be Barney Willow. A human for ever! Don't you see? I only want what's best for you.'

'No,' Maurice said, 'I don't see. Sorry, Mum, but I don't.'

The truth was, Maurice wanted to be a cat again, especially as now he knew he wouldn't have to live with Gavin, and his mother's words were only accelerating the change.

He fell forward, onto all fours, and shrank inside Barney's clothes.

Barney, meanwhile, was discovering you could wish through pain and that, indeed, pain is the wind in a wish's sails. And he wished so impossibly hard to be a human, to be himself, to be Barney Willow again, that the wooden chest shook beneath him, and his patch switched eyes, and the world became more vivid and alive, and he could feel his legs stretch and bend off the edge of the wooden chest. He felt dizzy, but he was still aware that his arms too were becoming human, losing their hair, gaining elbows, freckles. And, as his paws started to grow fingers, he grabbed Miss Whipmire's wrists and joined with his mum, his best friend, his dog – and even his cat-father, swiping her ankles – in wrestling her away from his increasingly human self.

In fact, Barney was so completely back inside his own body that when the police car arrived outside their house – the police car Sheila at number 33 had just called for – the policeman inside saw nothing except a psychotic head teacher trying to strangle a twelve-year-old boy wearing no clothes.

And no matter what the circumstances, that never looks particularly good.

The (Almost Completely) Happy Ending

Miss Whipmire was escorted to the police car as Rissa rescued Barney's clothes and Maurice the cat from the pavement.

Barney felt a bit embarrassed but Rissa promised to look away as he took the clothes and hurriedly carried them upstairs to his bedroom. *His* bedroom. *His* clothes.

The policemen had questions, obviously, but Barney just told them the truth, or a slice of the truth. That is, that Miss Whipmire was a bully who wanted to kill him for some reason.

Meanwhile, Miss Whipmire just sat miserable and handcuffed in the back of the police car, wishing, for the first time since her transformation, that she was a cat again. But it didn't matter how strongly she wished it, as the only cat she could now become was a pen pot, so Miss Whipmire had to stay human and would be locked away for a very long time.

As for Maurice, well, he found a new home. The Fairweathers wanted a cat, and Maurice fit the bill perfectly. Rissa and her parents kept him warm, fed him delicious carrot cake, and wrote a brilliant song about him called 'Maurice, the Cat Who Wanted to Be a Cat'. (OK, it wasn't *that* brilliant, but Maurice liked it very much, and even tried to miaow along to the chorus.)

Oh, and let's not forget Barney's dad. Well, the former plant salesman stayed a cat. I know, that's a bit sad. But that's what life is like sometimes. It has bits of sadness in it, splinters in the happiness. And Barney's life was no different.

He'd have liked his dad to be human again. Of course he would. But the most important thing was that he had his dad back. And living with them too, downstairs in his very own basket, chatting away to Guster. But still making a daily visit to the old lady on Friary Road who had looked after him so well, and still liked to spoil him.

And also, the really interesting thing was that now Barney's mum and dad got on better than ever before, and Neil Willow loved eating the apple and blackberry crumble she made for him every night. Plus, he loved spending time in the garden, sniffing the flowers he'd

once planted, and the ones Barney and his mum planted for him. Daffodils, bluebells, geraniums.

Petra and Petula kept on pursuing the nice former cat who was in Mr Willow's body, and eventually made the front page of the *Blandford Gazette* with their highly praised article which had the headline: CATTERY OWNER EATS CAT FOOD AND SLEEPS IN BASKET!

Barney's school life also underwent a great improvement.

Gavin was now too busy being laughed at by his former friends to do any bullying of his own. And, although Gavin's mum was a bit upset that her cat never came back, she decided to get a new one. Not until Florence was old enough to appreciate it. Which was also why they eventually gave up poor Leonard too, to a dog-loving ex-security guard who lived on their street.

Plus, the new head teacher, Mrs Raffles, turned out to be a very nice woman, and one who thought it was best if Barney's actual teachers marked his work.

Barney ended up with quite a lot of friends, but through it, Rissa remained his truest and best – even if it was sometimes annoying first thing in the morning to have her lean in close to his face and say, 'Yep, still you.'

People thought they were boyfriend and girlfriend,

and sometimes people would joke about that, but Barney didn't seem to be bothered if people laughed at him or not. Not any more. He was who he was. Take it or leave it. Anyway, Barney and Rissa were perfectly happy just being friends. Or that's what Barney was happy to accept. But if there was one thing Barney knew, it was that life doesn't stay still.

Indeed, two weeks later, Rissa asked Barney to the cinema. She said she wanted to see a 3D film about alien robots taking over the planet. It didn't sound very Rissa, so Barney got suspicious.

'What, on a date?'

Rissa shrugged. 'Call it what you want, cat-boy.'

And Barney felt that old familiar heat flush his cheeks, almost causing him to wish he had a face full of cat fur to hide it – but he obviously stopped himself wishing too hard.

'Yes. Course. It will be great. What should I wear? Should I act differently, you know, if it's a date?'

'No,' she said, smiling. 'I just want you to be you. Barney Willow.'

The evening of the date, as his dad and Guster sat watching proudly from the rug, Barney looked at his reflection in the mirror in his bedroom. His hair might have been a little on the wavy side. And he still had too

many freckles, and his ears still stuck out a bit too far –
although to be fair he didn't have old ladies squeezing
his cheeks these days. Yet, all put together, the person
staring back at Barney was a perfectly average but
totally unique boy, full of the thousand hopes and fears
that made him human. A boy who had no idea what
would happen in his life, or where it would take him.
One thing he was sure of was this – he would always
try and be *himself*.

And, as he went downstairs to put on his coat,
Barney couldn't think of anything in the world he'd
rather be.

The Bit After the End in Which the Author Has to Have the Last Word

So, there we are. The happy ending. I love a happy ending. It makes me feel all warm and cosy inside. Like those hot-water bottles you get which have their own woolly covers. Especially when the happy ending is part of a true story.

And yes, this is a true story. The world is full of humans who used to be cats and cats who used to be humans. So, the next time you see a cat looking up at you with those pleading eyes and that strong purr, just remember – it might want to jump into your life, rather than jump onto your lap.

But don't worry.

You'll be fine. Look at you. You are brilliant. A human being with – AHEM – incredible taste in books. No wonder all those cats who have wanted to be you have failed. Every day that you wake up as yourself and see that genius in the mirror is another reason to stay happy.

Well done you! No, seriously, well done. Right, I'd better go as I'm a bit sleepy and fancy a ~~nap by the radiator~~ sleep in my bed.

Yours truly,

~~Cat~~ Matt Haig